"Even though I like you and trust you with Brandon, the truth is we've only known each other a short time," Michelle said

"I've trusted people in the past, and had them let me down. I know I can't let those times color the rest of my life, but it's hard. The heart's not as resilient as the head thinks it should be."

Daniel wanted to stay mad at her, but he knew if Brandon was his and someone came into his life, he'd be as cautious as Michelle. "You're right. We both want what's best for Brandon. We're both reasonable people. I still maintain liking each other isn't another complication. And even if it is, I can't just stop liking you just because you think it would be more convenient."

"Me either." She stood on tiptoe and kissed his cheek—just the slightest peck. "You're very easy to like, Daniel McLean, darn it all."

He smiled, leaned down and kissed her on the cheek, as well. "You, too, Michelle Hamilton."

Two platonic kisses.

That's all they'd h

That's all there

But it wasn't.

Dear Reader,

Friendship. I've been very lucky to have some deep abiding friendships. Of course, since so many of my friends are other writers who live all over the world, my kids refer to them as my "invisible friends." But whether I see them every week or only see them now and again, I realize what a true gift they are. They make me laugh, support me when I need it and enrich my life in so many ways.

My heroine Michelle Hamilton works in a male-dominated office, and is so busy raising her nephew Brandon, she doesn't have time to form strong friendships or even date. She's content with her life. Yet when she gets "volunteered" to be on the PTA's social planning committee, she doesn't realize she'll be discovering two of the best friends any woman could ask for. And when her nephew begins a search for his biological father, she doesn't have an inkling Daniel McLean might be something so much more than a possible dad for Brandon.

Watching these three people come together and discover they're a family was a real holiday treat for me. No matter what holiday you celebrate, I hope it's one filled with family, friends and lots of love!

Holly

Once Upon a Christmas
HOLLY JACOBS

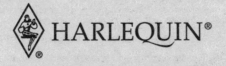

TORONTO • NEW YORK • LONDON
AMSTERDAM • PARIS • SYDNEY • HAMBURG
STOCKHOLM • ATHENS • TOKYO • MILAN • MADRID
PRAGUE • WARSAW • BUDAPEST • AUCKLAND

ISBN-13: 978-0-373-75242-3
ISBN-10:   0-373-75242-3

ONCE UPON A CHRISTMAS

Copyright © 2008 by Holly Fuhrmann.

www.eHarlequin.com

Printed in U.S.A.

ABOUT THE AUTHOR

In 2000, Holly Jacobs sold her first book to Harlequin Enterprises. She's since sold more than twenty novels to the publisher. Her romances have won numerous awards and made the Waldenbooks bestseller list. In 2005, Holly won a prestigious Career Achievement Award from *Romantic Times BOOKreviews*. In her nonwriting life Holly is married to a police lieutenant, and together they have four children. Visit Holly at www.HollyJacobs.com, or you can snail-mail her at P.O. Box 11102, Erie, PA 16514-1102.

Books by Holly Jacobs

Don't miss any of our special offers. Write to us at the following address for information on our newest releases.

Harlequin Reader Service
U.S.: 3010 Walden Ave., P.O. Box 1325, Buffalo, NY 14269
Canadian: P.O. Box 609, Fort Erie, Ont. L2A 5X3

For Deanne, who might live on the other side of the country, but is a true and valued friend.

Prologue

Michelle Hamilton practically crawled out of the bathroom and flopped onto the bed.

Normally, in her newly decorated room, snuggling under the duvet that matched the curtains, which coordinated with the half dozen throw pillows, gave her a sense of comfort and accomplishment.

This morning, she barely noticed the loveliness because she was so lost in her misery.

Michelle Hamilton was not often laid low by illness. Any illness. She couldn't remember the last time she was sick, and she hated the feeling of helplessness.

Another wave of nauseousness made her forget railing against her illness—it made her forget practically everything as she simply concentrated on calming her more than queasy stomach.

"Aunt Shell, are you driving me to school?" Brandon called through her closed bedroom door.

Drive?

Her stomach did another somersault. Lying on the bed rather

than the bathroom floor was almost too iffy for her fragile digestive tract to manage.

"Could you call Mrs. Ericson and ask if you can have a ride?" She tried to infuse something akin to life into her voice.

Her bedroom door opened slowly and timidly, and Brandon looked in.

In spite of her current illness, Michelle couldn't help but revel in the wonderment that this tall, gangly, rusty-haired boy on the verge of manhood was her nephew.

"You're sick?" he asked, concern in his expression.

She didn't try to answer, just nodded her head, which might have been a mistake. She put a hand on her stomach, as if she could hold the queasiness at bay.

"I could stay home with you," he offered.

She didn't risk shaking her head. Instead, she said, "No. I'm never sick, so I'm sure I'll be over this and feeling human before you get home from school."

Brandon didn't look convinced. "Okay, but I'll leave my cell on vibrate. Call if you need me."

She knew having a cell phone on was against school policy, but he was such a sweetheart, she didn't even argue it. Despite another wave of nauseousness, she smiled. "Thanks, honey, I will."

He'd no sooner shut the door than the phone on her bedside stand rang. Out of a Pavlovish sort of need to respond to a stimulus, she automatically reached over and picked up the receiver.

"Hello." Her voice sounded more like a croak than a proper salutation.

"Gee, Michelle, you sound horrible. I guess you missed the PTA meeting last night because you were sick? I mean, that never even occurred to me, since you're never sick."

"Heidi?" she asked, pretty sure she recognized her friend's voice.

"Yes. Listen, had I known you were sick and not just skipping, I'd have protected you. But…" The permanently perky PTA president hesitated. "Well, you know what happens when you miss a meeting, and the committee really needed volunteers, so when your name was suggested, I didn't step in—"

"What committee did they nominate me—" She interrupted herself with a groan. It was more a groan of pain from the illness than pain from working on a committee. She tried to be as active as possible in the school's activities. Brandon was in seventh grade. After next year, he'd be on to high school. She wanted to savor and remember every moment of his childhood. So, ultimately, it didn't matter what committee she was on. Even if she'd made the meeting, she'd have probably volunteered for it.

"You're on the—" Heidi started.

The waves intensified into a tsunami and Michelle eased herself off the bed.

"Just send me the stuff, Heidi," she said, and simply dropped the phone as she sprinted the last few steps to the master bathroom.

Within seconds she forgot all about Heidi's call.

Chapter One

November

Michelle straightened her skirt as she got out of her very sensible car. She'd bought it because it was safe and fuel efficient. She'd intended to buy a white one, since she'd read white cars didn't show dirt as readily as other colors. But for some reason, when she was talking to the dealer, she hadn't pointed to the white car, but rather to the burnt-orange one. The color made her think of autumn leaves. She unconsciously patted the car as she got out in front of Erie Elementary.

The school was a two-story brick building with a row of oaks lining the path to the building and twin maple trees flanking the entry. The trees had been awash with autumn colors just a few weeks ago, but now only the most tenacious leaves clung to their otherwise barren branches. There was a definite nip in the air, proclaiming snow would be coming soon. And once snow started falling in Erie, Pennsylvania, it didn't stop until March…sometimes even April.

By then, the meetings of the PTA's Social Planning Committee would be over. Michelle didn't feel a surge of relief at the thought. She'd miss seeing Samantha Williams and Carly

Lewis every other Friday. Together, the three of them were the Social Planning Committee.

Shaking off her sense of foreboding, Michelle walked toward the well-lit entryway. Samantha, in charge of the Thanksgiving Pageant, always commented on how much she enjoyed coming into the dark, quiet school. But Michelle didn't enjoy it. As a matter of fact, she liked the school during the day when it bustled with kids and energy.

Still, she did look forward to these meetings.

Tonight's centered on making sure they had everything ready for the Thanksgiving Pageant, after which they'd assess what needed to be done for next month's Christmas Fair. There were crafts and gifts to attend to, volunteers to organize, games to repair or rebuild and even a Santa to be rented. Michelle was in charge of the Christmas event, but she wasn't anxious. She thrived on creating order from chaos.

However, neither the Thanksgiving Pageant nor the Christmas Fair was what was on her mind as she entered the school. It was Samantha and Carly. For years, she'd known them both in a peripheral way because Erie Elementary was small enough that she was aware of most parents on at least a nod-to basis. But since they'd been thrown onto the Social Planning Committee together, they'd become more than just two fellow PTA parents…they'd become friends.

And tonight Michelle really needed friends.

Carly Lewis was already in the meeting room when Michelle walked in. Normally, the petite, black-haired woman's slightly upturned eyes would crinkle as she smiled, but tonight there was no crinkle because there was no smiling welcome.

"You'll never guess what happened this week," they said in unison.

"You want to start?" Michelle asked.

"We'd better wait for Samantha." Carly patted the seat next to her. "She's bringing the snack, and I'm hoping whatever it is contains chocolate. I can guarantee that this is a chocolate sort of night."

"I—" Michelle didn't get any further because Samantha Williams joined them.

"You'll never guess what happened this week." Samantha set a box resembling an egg carton on the table then took off her coat. The mother of four sounded tired as she brushed her brown hair out of her eyes.

"That's what I said earlier," Carly said, sounding depressed.

"Me, too." Michelle eyed the box. Chocolate-covered strawberries from Pulakos, if she wasn't mistaken. She hoped she wasn't mistaken, because she shared Carly's feeling that tonight was a chocolate sort of night. "We waited for you before we started spilling."

"You guys start, then I'll tell you my news." Samantha opened the box and it was indeed chocolate-covered strawberries. She took one and nibbled at the end.

Carly took one, as well. "Michelle first."

"It's Brandon," she blurted out. "He wants to find his father."

He'd come to her last night looking nervous. As he sat down next to her on the couch she'd known immediately that something was wrong.

"Aunt Shell?" he'd said tentatively.

"What is it, honey?"

Her concern had been validated when he didn't teasingly remind her that she was supposed to call him Brandon, not *honey, sweetie,* or *love.* "Aunt Shell, I want to know who my father is."

She'd expected to hear about a bad grade in school—and a bad grade in Brandon's eyes was anything less than an A, despite her assurance that an occasional B wasn't going to keep him out of the college of his choice. Brandon was a serious student. A serious boy.

Maybe that was her fault. She'd come into parenting her nephew so unexpectedly. She'd read everything she could, but she'd never encountered a situation like this in any of the how-to books.

"Bran, I don't—" How could she tell him she didn't know? That her sister, Tara, his mother, had had a long line of boyfriends when she lived at home, and after she left—well, she hadn't talked to Michelle about things like boyfriends when she made her infrequent calls. Hell, she hadn't even told Michelle about Brandon until the day Tara had shown up on Michelle's doorstep five years ago with the eight-year-old in tow. She'd refused to talk about Brandon's father, even after she revealed that she was dying. Tara simply said Brandon was hers—and hers alone.

"Bran, honey, I don't know who your father is," she'd said. The look on his face would haunt her for some time.

Michelle shook off the memory. Samantha and Carly were both waiting for her to continue, but Michelle didn't know what to say. How did you admit your own sister had disappeared from your life for almost a decade, only to return when she was too sick to continue to care for her son on her own?

"You don't know where his father is?" Carly asked, a gentleness in her voice that showed off the soft side she rarely displayed.

"I don't know *who* his father is," Michelle admitted, "much less where he is."

Neither of her friends said anything. Michelle couldn't blame them. What was there to say to a statement like that? Her sister had hurt her in so many ways, but not telling her about

Brandon, and not leaving her with answers to help him now, made the rest of the pain seem insignificant. Deciding how to handle his questions about his father was tearing her up.

"That's the problem. What if I help Brandon find the man, and he's…" She hesitated. "What if he's not the kind of man you'd want in a young boy's life? I met some of my sister Tara's boyfriends and, believe me, there's a very good possibility that's the case. What if we find him and he hurts Brandon? Not physically. I'd never let that happen. But what if he tells him he doesn't want him? Or what if…" Her voice dropped to hardly more than a whisper. "What if he wants full custody? I could lose Brandon."

"Oh, Michelle." Samantha patted her hand.

Michelle studied the two women. She had known she could count on their support. That meant so much. She worked in a male-dominated office. She wasn't sure if it was that women were less likely to major in accounting, or if A&D Financial didn't hire many women, but in any event, she was the only woman in her office. She didn't mind hanging out with the guys, but none of them were friends. And though Heidi was her friend, Heidi's life was perfect and orderly. She was happily married and just seemed to radiate contentment. Michelle didn't think Heidi could really relate to something this…well, messy.

Maybe that was part of the bond she had with Samantha and Carly. They were single moms, dealing with all the messiness of balancing kids and jobs on their own. Michelle might be Brandon's aunt, but she felt a kinship with her PTA mom friends. With Samantha and Carly she could let it all hang out.

"Brandon came to live with me right after I graduated from college. Part of me hoped someone else would claim him. My mom. His father. I was young and I didn't know the first thing about raising a child. But now, he's my life. My sister made a lot of mistakes, and I couldn't do anything to stop her. But Brandon was her greatest achievement and she trusted him to me. How can I live without him? He needs me. And I need him. Maybe that's selfish, but I don't know who I'd be if I wasn't Brandon's aunt."

Carly leaned over and hugged Michelle. Touchy-feely wasn't the norm for Carly, which made the gesture even more treasured.

"No matter what happens," Carly assured her, "you'll always be his aunt. He'll always love you."

"How can I take that risk? How can I help him find someone neither of us knows and take a chance that I'll lose everything to him?"

Samantha nodded. "What did you tell Brandon?"

"I told him we'd wait. When he's eighteen I'll do everything in my power to help him find his father."

"How'd he take that?" Carly asked.

The pain of his reaction was still fresh for Michelle. "He was furious. He's still hardly talking to me. And Bran and I don't fight like that. I don't know how to handle it…to handle him."

"He knows you love him and he'll come around," Samantha promised her. "We've had our own hurdles at my house, but the kids know I love them, and that's why they always get over being mad. So will Brandon."

"I hope so." Michelle didn't feel very confident that Brandon was going to just *get over* this. "I hope our talk was the end of it. I hate having him mad at me, and feeling as if I've somehow let him down."

Carly and Samantha continued comforting Michelle, and she let them. She needed to hear that everything was going to be all right. Even if she wasn't sure she believed it.

But she could see something in Carly's face, something that

said she needed to vent, as well, so Michelle thanked Samantha and Carly. Then she pointed to Carly. "Your turn."

For a moment her friend hesitated. But Carly's need to unload was evident as she said in a burst, "Dean and I are trying to finish the divorce settlement with a mediator. As soon as that's worked out, it's all done. My marriage is over." She paused. "No, I take that back, the marriage was over the moment I caught him with his secretary on that couch I bought for his office. The actual divorce was in January, despite the fact we hadn't sorted out the marital assets. I graduate in December, and I'd really like to go into the new year with a degree, a new job and a totally finished divorce. I can't spare much more time for this. I've got a couple huge papers due, on top of getting ready for the start of the holiday season."

This time Michelle joined Samantha in making comforting noises as Carly continued to talk about her ex, and how he'd balked about paying for her to go back to school, despite the fact she'd quit college to put him through law school.

As Carly wound down, she joined Michelle in looking at Samantha. That's all it took for their friend to blurt out, "I broke off my friendship with Harry."

Samantha had been growing closer and closer to Erie Elementary's interim principal, Harry Remington. She'd claimed that they were simply friends, but Michelle and Carly had talked about it, and neither had bought Samantha's definition of their relationship. It was clear to them, if not to Samantha, that there was more than a friendship brewing between the two of them.

As Samantha told them she'd kissed Harry, Michelle shot Carly a private smile behind Samantha's back. Their suspicions were verified. But then Samantha said that her oldest, Stan, was having trouble accepting her friendship with Harry.

"So, I ended it. I'm sure it's for the best. He's leaving soon, anyway."

That did surprise Michelle. Samantha didn't seem like the type who'd give up something she wanted without a fight. "And you didn't want to."

"No, I didn't want to, but right now, the kids have to come first. Stan has to come first."

The fact that Samantha would put her own wants and desires aside for her kids didn't surprise Michelle, either. Samantha was an unselfish, loving mother.

Was Michelle being selfish by denying Brandon her help in searching for his father?

Was it concern for her nephew or a selfish fear of losing him that had prompted her response?

She wasn't sure. And she didn't want to think about it, so she said, "We're supposed to talk about the Thanksgiving Pageant. Is there anything we can do?"

Samantha shook her head. "No, there's nothing either of you need to worry about. I've got it all under control."

Michelle wished she could say the same.

She'd built a solid life for herself and her nephew. A good life.

Brandon had spent his first eight years living a vagabond existence with Tara. Moving from place to place, while her sister moved from man to man. Always searching for something. For someone.

Yet maybe Michelle's life was too regimented. Maybe what she thought was a comforting sense of order had left Brandon feeling smothered and stifled. Maybe that's why he wanted to find his father, to find a way out.

She sat, eating chocolate-covered strawberries, and worried that somehow she'd messed up and that her nephew was going to be left to pay the price.

DANIEL MCLEAN CLOSED the shop door and walked the dozen or so steps through his backyard to his house's back porch, wading through what was left of the foot of snow that had fallen the day after Thanksgiving. This weekend had been warmer, reducing the snow to a troublesome slush in the yard.

He kicked off his boots next to the door and walked into the kitchen. He stood a moment and took it in. The cabinets he'd spent last winter working on between jobs looked perfect. Their deep maple hue gave the room a warm feeling. Once he finished the mantelpiece he was carving, this room would be done. Then it was on to the library.

He'd bought the old house last year. It was perfectly situated on a small wooded lot just outside Erie in Greene Township. He had neighbors who were close enough if he needed a hand, but not in eyesight of the house. Making the old barn in back into a workshop had been his first project. The house was going to take longer, mainly because it wasn't a priority. Work had to come first.

McLean's Restoration had taken off. He was booked for the next nine months.

He opened the fridge and took out a can of soda. He'd just popped the tab when the doorbell rang.

A spurt of anticipation surged through him. It had to be the triple iron complex cabinet molder he'd ordered from Scotland. Scanning antique tool sites was one of his hobbies. He didn't feel guilty about his passion for old, authentic tools because not only did using them on projects add authenticity to his work, they were a tax write-off.

Smiling, he opened the door, expecting to see the brown uniform of the delivery man, Rich.

Instead, a gangly teen with rust-colored hair stood looking as if he was going to throw up.

"You okay?" Daniel asked.

"Are you Daniel McLean?" the kid countered, standing up straighter.

"Yes. Can I help you?"

"Did you go to Penn State about thirteen years ago?"

Daniel did a quick mental math problem and realized it had been that long ago. Only eleven years since he graduated, but still over a decade since he'd been in college. On one hand, that sounded like a long time. On the other, he felt rather proud at how well the business was doing. "Yes. What's this all about?"

"Did you know a Tara Hamilton?"

The kid wasn't very good at answering questions. But talk about a blast from the past.

Tara Hamilton had been a waitress at a local café. He could still see her wearing her short skirt and apron, smiling as she handed out food and drinks. They'd become friends his freshman year and, for one brief moment, right after the holidays in his sophomore year, he'd thought that maybe they'd become more….

He shook himself from his reverie. "Yes. I knew Tara."

The boy extended his hand. "I'm her son, Brandon Hamilton, and I was wondering if you could be my dad."

The boy turned deathly pale at the words, but he held his ground.

It was Daniel who felt as if the world wobbled beneath him. "Did you ask Tara—your mom?"

"She's dead." The boy's answer was flat and matter-of-fact.

Daniel's world shifted again. He'd thought of Tara over the past thirteen years. She'd been so instrumental in propelling him toward his own dreams and not someone else's expectations. Each small success as he'd built his business had brought her to mind.

They'd bonded over the fact they'd both been from Erie. It

might have been only a three-and-a-half-hour drive between there and school, but to a homesick college student it had seemed a world away. Tara had been a tangible connection to home, to the familiar, at first. Later, she'd been a friend. And for that one night, she'd been his. That next morning, Daniel had thought there was potential for a true and lasting relationship, but Tara had left.

He'd eventually come to terms with the fact no one would ever clip free-flying Tara's wings. When he thought about her, he imagined her in exotic ports, backpacking through Europe. A hippie in an age of yuppies.

But dead?

The thought shook him in a way that thirteen years of separation shouldn't have allowed.

"How long?" he managed.

"Five years," the boy said.

What was his name?

Brandon. It was Brandon.

"She's been gone five years," Daniel said aloud, wondering if that would make it seem more real. It did, and the pain, despite the decade-plus of separation, was acute. "And your father…"

"She never told me who he was. But I went into the attic and found her stuff. There was a program for some Penn State art show, with your name highlighted. And she gave me this when I was little."

Brandon dangled a silver medal from a chain. Saint Joseph.

Daniel unconsciously touched his neck. That medal had hung there for only a year. His grandmother had given it to him before he left for college. His grandfather had insisted that Daniel pursue a business degree. *Make something of yourself, son. Don't live hand-to-mouth like we have,* he'd said over and over. But his grandmother had known he wanted nothing more than to follow in his grandfather's footsteps and turn his carpentry hobby into a career. *Saint Joseph was a carpenter,* she'd said. *Maybe he can show you the way.*

Maybe in a way he had, through Tara. That's why he'd given the medal to her. He'd slipped it from his neck and onto hers and told her, "You've shown me my dream, now maybe he'll help you find yours." She'd kissed him for the first time, then. She'd kissed him before, in a friendly way, but this kiss had spoken of intimate things. He'd taken her to bed, and started to consider the possibility of a future together. In the end, he hadn't been surprised that Tara's dreams hadn't led to a life with him.

"It says D. McLean on the back," said the boy.

Daniel realized they were still standing in the doorway. He threw the door open wider. "Maybe you'd better come in."

The boy shook his head. "My aunt's going to kill me as it is. Going into a stranger's house would only make her madder. But we could sit on the porch."

Daniel nodded. His brain had gone fuzzy. He wasn't sure what to say to this kid—Brandon. Tara's son. Maybe his? He slipped on a pair of sneakers.

"So?" the boy demanded as he sat gingerly on the edge of one of the rocking chairs Daniel had made. "Are you?"

Daniel sank into the chair next to him. "Son—Brandon, I did know your mother. We were friends for a couple years. Good friends. And I guess there's a chance that I could be your father, but it's a remote chance at best. How old are you? When's your birthday?"

"I turned thirteen at the end of September. I should be in eighth grade, but Mom and I moved around so much, Aunt Shell held me back."

The timing wasn't wrong. But when he'd known her, Tara had

gone through multiple boyfriends, one she'd broken up with not long before they had their very brief fling. He almost laughed at the phrase. Brief fling? One night was as brief as flings could get.

He tried to remember the name of that last guy Tara had dated, but couldn't. What he did remember was Tara's laughter. She'd always been laughing at everything, as if she were full of so much joy she had to let some of it out so she didn't explode from it. Her laughter bubbled over. At a time when Daniel had felt at odds with the world, that sound was a salve, soothing him like nothing else could.

He'd felt the lack when she'd left. She hadn't told him where she was going, and there was no note of explanation. Nothing.

For a long time he'd waited, hoping she'd be back, or at least call. Having witnessed the demise of more than a few of her relationships, he should have known better. When Tara broke it off with a guy, she severed things completely.

He wasn't sure what, if anything, to say to this boy who was studying him intently. Brandon had soft brown eyes, and the stubborn cowlick at the crown of his head sent his rusty hair going in too many directions at once.

Tara had been from Erie. That first day he'd met her in the diner, they'd talked and found they shared this city as a connection. After he'd moved home, he'd always fantasized that someday he'd pass her on the street, or spot her at the mall, or having coffee. All these years he'd lived with that possibility.

But she was dead.

He'd never bump into her and hear her laughter as they talked over old times.

The pain was intense.

"Brandon, you mentioned an aunt?" He seemed to vaguely recall Tara talking about having a sister.

The boy nodded. "My aunt Shell. I live with her since Mom…"

"And this aunt doesn't know you're here?" he asked, though he realized, from the boy's comment about not coming into the house, she couldn't know.

Brandon confirmed that when he shook his head.

"Listen, I think I should talk to your aunt."

"She didn't want me looking for my father. She'll be mad."

"Like I said, there's a chance you are my son." Saying the words felt foreign. A son. Even if it was the remotest of chances, it was there. This boy might be his son. His and Tara's. Daniel couldn't walk away from that. He wouldn't.

"If you're mine that means your aunt will find out eventually. Would you want to spring it on her? Or give her a chance to get used to it while it's still only a possibility?"

"Aunt Shell doesn't do springing." He sighed. "Okay, we should talk to her." He gave Daniel an address on Erie's east side.

"Want to toss your bike in the truck and ride with me?"

"Nah, she's going to be upset regardless. I'm not getting in a car with a stranger and making it worse. I'll ride my bike and meet you there."

"It's quite a haul back into town and it's freezing out." Daniel's place was about five miles from the city of Erie proper. And Erie in November was cold. Today was in the low forties, a bone-chilling ride on a bike.

"I made it out here, I can make it back," Brandon said firmly.

"Fine. Just let me get my keys then." Daniel started toward the house, then turned around and drank in the sight of the boy, searching his features for some sense of the familiar, some sign that this Brandon was his son.

"Mr. McLean, what if you are my father? How are you going to feel?" There was vulnerability in the question.

Daniel wasn't sure how he'd feel, but he could see that

Brandon needed something, so he said, "I'll confess, this is out of the blue, and I haven't thought about having kids, but if I'm your father, then I can promise you I'll want to be a part of your life. We'll have to wait and see how. Your aunt will have something to say about that, I'm sure."

Daniel knew what it was like to be abandoned, to feel as if you didn't matter. Nothing, and no one, not even this Aunt Shell, would keep him away from the boy if he was Brandon's father. He'd have to make that clear right from the start. He didn't want to disrupt their lives, but he wouldn't be shut out, either.

Brandon offered him a timid smile. "Uh, sir, I mean, Mr. McLean, my aunt will definitely have something to say, and I'm pretty sure most of it is going to be aimed at me."

Daniel paused. "She doesn't…" He wanted to ask, needed to know that Tara's son wasn't being abused, but he didn't know how to ask.

Brandon must have caught his meaning. "No. Nothing like that. My aunt loves me, and would do anything to protect me, even if that means trying to protect me from myself."

"Or from me?"

"You, too. She's afraid that looking for my father might end up hurting me. Mom didn't always have the nicest boyfriends, and Aunt Shell is afraid that my father might be someone who could hurt me. But I had to know, even if it hurts." That said, Brandon got his bike, climbed on it and pedaled down the driveway and onto the street.

Daniel moved as if in a fog. In the house, he grabbed his keys and wallet, then got in the truck and followed him. He passed Brandon on Old Wattsburg Road, before he passed the top of Kirsch Road.

He glanced in the rearview mirror at the boy pedaling madly.

A son?

Would Tara have had a baby and kept it from him? He'd love to be able to say unequivocally no, but he couldn't. Tara had been…well, Tara.

He felt a wave of sorrow over the loss of his friend, even though it had been more than a decade since he'd seen her.

A son?

He kept circling the idea.

A son?

A thirteen-year-old son?

Suddenly, he was furious. The speed at which he went from mourning to anger took his breath away. If Tara had been pregnant with his child and hadn't contacted him…

He realized there was nothing he'd be able to do about it now.

He let out a long breath, strangely deflated and a little numb. What should he do?

He'd meet up with this *Aunt Shell* and tell her what? That he'd slept with her sister exactly once and didn't have a clue if he could be Brandon's father. When she asked what he wanted to do about it, what would he say?

He needed to know if he was Brandon's father. That much was clear. And obviously, Brandon wanted the same thing.

After that? If Brandon was his son, then he'd want to be with him. He wasn't sure in what capacity, but he'd want to spend time with him and help out financially. He'd make sure that Brandon knew Daniel hadn't abandoned him. That if he'd known he had a son, he'd have done whatever it took to be a part of his life for his first thirteen years.

Since Daniel couldn't go back and do that, he'd do whatever it would take to play some role in his life now.

He'd try to give Aunt Shell—who didn't do springing—

some time to adjust, but he'd be frank. One way or another, if he was Brandon's father, he was going to be part of both their lives from here on out.

Chapter Two

Daniel drove slowly down the street, checking the numbers on the houses. He pulled up in front of a small, brick home in a nice, middle-class neighborhood. There were flower beds in the front, now covered with a mixture of slushy snow and leaves from the big maple tree that stood on the eastern side of the property.

Everything about the house was…precise. That was the word to describe this house. A very symmetrical arrangement of bushes on either side of the porch steps. The inch or so of snow sat lightly on the grass but was brushed off the sidewalk and stairs. A grapevine wreath, decorated with red flowers, sat centered on the door. All the blinds in the window were pulled halfway up, with no deviation.

Precise.

The whole exterior of this house spoke of someone who liked things neat and orderly.

The fact that Daniel was here was going to disturb Brandon's aunt Shell's order. Daniel knew he had no choice—he had to know whether Brandon was his son—but it didn't stop him from feeling bad about shocking the woman.

He could wait for Brandon. He was pretty sure that's what the boy expected. Daniel could see him standing on Daniel's front porch, so scared and yet so determined. Brandon would face his aunt's anger head-on.

But Daniel wasn't about to hide behind a boy. He'd go up and introduce himself, take the brunt of this woman's anger.

Tara's sister.

Brandon's aunt and guardian.

Daniel got out of the truck and went to the front door. He rang the bell.

Moments later, a tall blonde opened the door and smiled pleasantly. She wasn't what he'd expected. Tara had been shorter. Her hair color was subject to change. One day pink, another brown. She'd had piercings and tattoos, been wild and unpredictable.

This woman wasn't, if appearances were correct. She wore a simple pair of navy slacks and a blouse. A single teardrop pearl hung from a gold chain. Her hair was in a neat bun, and if she was wearing makeup it was light enough that he couldn't tell.

Her smile faded as he took a bit too long assessing her. "Yes? Can I help you?"

"Are you Brandon Hamilton's aunt?"

She nodded, smiling again. "Michelle Hamilton. And you are?"

Ah, he had thought maybe Shell was short for Shelly, but instead it was short for Michelle.

"My name's Daniel McLean. I'm an old friend of Tara's."

The smile vanished and a look of wariness replaced it. "Yes?" she asked, more cautiously this time.

"Your nephew showed up at my door today, with an old medal of mine, asking if I could be his father."

The woman's pale skin lightened further, leaving her a waxy ghost.

"I don't want to cause you any trouble," he assured her, hoping to allay some of her obvious fear, "but the truth is, he could be mine. We need to talk about that."

For a moment, she stood mute, but then an expression, very much like Brandon's when Daniel had opened the front door, settled in. "No, we don't. I'm Brandon's legal guardian, and—"

"And you know him well enough to understand that he won't let this go. Hell, I've just met him and already know as much. The fact is, you don't know me yet, but let me assure you, I won't let it go, either."

"Mr. McLean, was it?"

He nodded.

"I don't take threats lightly."

"It's not a threat, it's just me telling you how it is. There's an equally likely chance I'm not his father. Tara and I—" He stopped a moment, a fresh wave of anger at his old friend washing over him. "We just had one night, and then she left without a word."

"Tara was famous for that," Michelle assured him with a tinge of bitterness in her tone that told him she had no illusions about Tara.

"She left and the timing was close enough that Brandon could be mine. I didn't want to say anything to him, but I do know she'd broken up with someone a few weeks before the two of us…were together. And I don't know who she was with after. So, I can't be sure."

"What do you want me to do? Are you suggesting I let one of Tara's one-night stands be a part of my nephew's life on the off chance he's his father? I can guarantee you that's not going to happen."

"It's true that Tara and I had just that one night together, but we were more than that. We'd been friends for two years. Good friends."

Daniel saw that Michelle's knuckles had turned white as she gripped the edge of the door even harder. "If you were such good friends, Mr. McLean, don't you think she'd have told you about Brandon if you were my nephew's father?"

He'd like to think so but, knowing Tara, he wasn't sure. "You know your sister. Is there a chance she wouldn't have told Brandon's father she was pregnant?" She visually flinched at the question. "Maybe we could talk inside?"

She looked reluctant, and he couldn't blame her. "Miss Hamilton—"

"Ms."

"Ms. Hamilton. I can understand your not wanting to invite me inside, but I think it might be preferable to having your neighbors in on our conversation. There's someone in the window of the house next door, blatantly watching, and a second ago, she unlocked the window, and—" his voice dropped and he leaned closer "—it just opened a crack."

She glanced over at the next house and forced a smile. "Hi, Mrs. Myers." Then she said, "You're right. Come in."

It was definitely not the most gracious invitation Daniel had ever received, but he couldn't blame her. He was a perfect stranger, and she was trying to protect Brandon.

She let him inside to a small entry hall. As she shut the door behind him, he noticed the shoe rack and the coat hooks. There was a small basket on the inside door handle, with letters in it. He assumed she'd be mailing them tomorrow.

He'd been right. This was a woman who liked things neat and tidy—precise.

"Where's Brandon?"

"He rode his bike out to my house. I hated the thought of him riding back into town, given the cold, but he insisted that he was already going to be in trouble with you and he wasn't going to add to it by coming inside my house or getting in my car. Part of me wished he'd have let me give him a ride. The other is impressed that you've taught him to be careful…safe."

She nodded, and he wasn't sure if she knew he'd meant that as a compliment. Of course, his complimentary skills were more than weak. He'd have to be more blatant next time.

"You might as well come have a seat while we wait for him."

Again, not exactly a heartfelt invitation, but Daniel would take what he could get.

Michelle Hamilton led him into a living room. It was comfortably furnished, and in keeping with the rest of the house. The deep brown couch had half a dozen throw pillows on it, but there was no throwing. They were evenly spaced and all completely straight. There were magazines on one end table, and they were neatly stacked. There was a small fireplace, with a fire already laid out and ready to go.

"Nice place." He meant it. Despite the fact she liked things in their assigned places—or maybe because of it—the room was inviting.

"Have a seat," she offered, sounding a bit more hospitable now.

Daniel sat on the couch, and she took one of the matching chairs opposite it.

"So, what are we going to do?" he asked.

"*We* are not going to do anything. I'm obviously going to have to do something, because I'm Brandon's aunt and his guardian. You are a stranger who has no rights whatsoever in this matter."

"A stranger who might be your nephew's father," he pointed out gently. "I need to know if I am, every bit as much as he wants to know. I'm going to suggest that's our first order of business."

"And if you are his father? What then? Where do you picture that leading, Mr. McLean?"

"Ms. Hamilton, we'll cross that bridge when we come to it."

MICHELLE WORKED at keeping her breathing even, worked on keeping her demeanor calm, because she was not going to give this stranger an inch.

This Daniel McLean, who'd admitted he'd had a one-night stand with her sister, couldn't walk into her home and tell her he planned on seeing if Brandon was his son, and if he was, then they'd *cross that bridge*.

Michelle was not the type of person who crossed any bridge unless she knew exactly what was on the other side. And no matter what was on the other side of this particular bridge, she was pretty sure she didn't want to cross it at all.

"Mr. McLean, I'm not prepared to do anything until I've consulted with a lawyer." She'd call Henry Rizzo from Erie Elementary, whose daughter, Izzy, was in second grade. They weren't exactly friends, but they were friendly and she was sure he'd help. There was a feeling of connection at Erie Elementary, even between families that only knew each other in passing.

"Do you really want to do that, Ms. Hamilton? Do you really want to turn this into a battle before we even know if I'm Brandon's father? Before you even know me?"

"I don't want to, Mr. McLean, but you're right, I don't know you. And I'm not willing to allow a perfect stranger—who's admitted he was just another one-night stand for Tara—to waltz into my home and try to tell me what we are and aren't going to do."

"Do you know who Brandon's father is? Maybe there's some reason you don't want him to know."

She could lie.

Michelle knew she could say yes. That she knew who Brandon's father was and that she was keeping it from Brandon because…because the man was in jail.

It was plausible.

It was tempting.

Tara probably wouldn't have hesitated lying to a stranger to protect herself, or to get what she wanted, but Michelle just couldn't do it.

"Mr. McLean, Tara left home the moment she turned eighteen." Her father had passed away when she was very young. Then her sister was gone. And finally, her mother remarried during Michelle's first year of college and started a new life, in a new state. A life that didn't include Michelle. Those losses were still fresh, all these years later.

"I'd get an occasional call from Tara every few months. Sometimes it was almost a year between calls. But she always did call. She'd ask about me, but she never said where she was or what she was doing, even when I asked. She'd just brush the question aside. Eventually, I stopped asking. Tara lived life on her own terms, without much care for anyone else's feelings. To be honest, she never even told me she had a son. I didn't know until she showed up on my doorstep, Brandon in tow."

Michelle could distinctly remember that moment. She'd opened her front door, and Tara was there, pale and sickly, with a small boy at her side. "This is your aunt, Brandon," Tara had said to the boy in his well-worn clothing, a tattered stuffed horse in his hand. Michelle hadn't missed Tara's meaning, and quickly became angry.

How could her sister not have told her?

The anger took a back seat when Tara announced she had cancer. It's hard to fight with someone whose second sentence was, "She'll be taking care of you after I die."

"Tara told me she was dying and that she'd brought Brandon to me to raise. My mom had remarried and already cut me out of her life, so she didn't want Brandon." Even now, her mother rarely visited or even called. "Tara never gave me the full story of where she'd been and what she'd been doing all those years. She just took care of the paperwork and two months after she'd arrived, she died."

Two months. That's all she'd had with her sister. The last few weeks Tara hadn't said much, not that she'd been good at saying the things that mattered when she still could. And it took months for Brandon to start opening up.

"From what Brandon's said, they moved from place to place, or more accurately, my sister moved from man to man, always looking for a better love. So, no, I never asked which of those men was Brandon's father. When Bran started asking, I promised to help him find out when he was eighteen. I don't suppose you'd be willing to wait until then?"

Daniel shook his head. "I don't suppose I would."

She sighed. "I didn't think so."

The front door flew open and Brandon, his cheeks red and chapped from the long bike ride in the cold, burst into the room. "You came."

"I told you I would," Daniel said softly.

"I wasn't sure." Brandon turned to Michelle. She could see his nervousness, but he stood tall and faced her. "I know you wanted me to wait, but I couldn't. I need to know who my father is. I'm old enough to make that decision. But if you're going to punish me, then I'll accept it, because even if you didn't specifically tell me I couldn't look for him now, we both know that you thought I was going to wait."

"So, you lied to me, and then you skipped out of basketball practice and rode your bike—"

"Out to Greene Township."

"You were riding your bike on Route Eight in the freezing cold? I'm supposed to take those as signs that you're mature enough to handle a decision this big?"

"I'm sorry about all of that, but I knew you wouldn't let me."

"I thought this was settled. If you wanted to impress me with how grown-up you are, you should have told me that it wasn't settled at all."

"I need to know, Aunt Shell." He glanced from her to Daniel McLean, longing evident in his expression.

Seeing it softened Michelle. "Just go to your room, Brandon, while I finish talking to Mr. McLean."

"I want to spend time with him."

"I know you do, but he's a stranger, and I'm not comfortable with that right now. Mr. McLean and I are trying to figure out—"

"He could be my dad. He said so. You can't make me stay away from him, Aunt Shell."

"Brandon, go to your room now," she said sharply. "We'll discuss this later."

Brandon glared at her with more anger visible in his expression than she'd ever seen before. He wheeled around and faced Daniel McLean. "Mr. McLean, no matter what my aunt says, I want to find out if you're my father. I want to know you and spend time with you." That said, Brandon wheeled around and stormed from the room. Michelle could hear his pounding steps up the stairs, followed by his bedroom door slamming.

"I think we'd better come up with some sort of plan, Ms. Hamilton, because your nephew appears to be a very determined boy. I don't think anything you do will dissuade him for long. And I'll confess, if I am his father, that particular characteristic might come from me, because although I can understand you need some time to process this, I won't be put off for long, either."

He stood. "I'll go now. You make any calls you need to, seek whatever advice you want, then contact me." He reached into his back pocket, pulled out a wallet, removed a card and handed it to her. "All my information's on that. I have my own business. I do finish carpentry. I'm working on a project for Christopher Brothers Construction right now. They're in the book. They'll vouch for me on a professional level."

"And on a personal one?"

"Ask for Josh. He'll vouch for me personally, as well. I think that will do for starters. I'll expect your call soon, Ms. Hamilton, because I want answers as much as your nephew does."

He turned and strode from her house.

Michelle heard the front door close and knew she should get up, knew she should do something. She should start a list of things to do. Talk to a lawyer. She wasn't sure what kind of law Henry Rizzo practiced, but he could give her a referral, give her some sort of place to start.

She should look up his number now.

She should call this Christopher Brothers Construction and ask for Josh.

She should go talk to Brandon.

She should…

But she didn't.

She simply sat and tried to think through her mind-numbing fear that someone was going to take Brandon away from her.

Of all the things she should do, that was the one thing she *had* to do. She had to protect her nephew.

Even if it meant protecting him from himself.

Feeling a sense of resolve, Michelle walked up the stairs and knocked on Brandon's bedroom door. There was a mumbled response that she took as an invitation to enter.

She opened the door and walked into the evening-gloomy room. She switched on the light and found Brandon sitting in the chair by the window.

"You made him leave." It was an accusation. Brandon glared at her.

The expression broke Michelle's heart. "Honey, I—"

"Aunt Shell, I know you think you're protecting me, but I'm thirteen. I'm growing up. And I deserve to know my father."

"Bran—"

"Do you know what it was like when Mom was alive?"

Brandon rarely talked about Tara. Oh, there were bits and pieces he'd let slip over the years. Michelle had asked, but he'd always been vague. "No, honey, I don't know much. Only what you told me."

"My mom was always laughing. Always smiling. Mom was always sure her next boyfriend would be the love of her life. She'd move us into his house and for the first few weeks things would be great. She'd tell me that she'd found me a new dad and tell me stories about the life we'd all have together. Fantastic stories about the fun we'd have. But, Aunt Shell, they were just stories."

Brandon sounded so mature.

No, so old and jaded. As if at thirteen he already was so much older than Tara had ever been.

"The longest we ever lived with anyone was with this guy named Johnson. He had a garage and he'd come home every night and smell of gasoline and oil. He'd pat me on the head and say, 'Hey, squirt,' then go in and shower before dinner. At first, Mom would have it all ready for him. Then later, Mom would call and say she was working late, and me and Johnson would get our own dinner. He taught me all about football, 'cause he liked it. And cars. He liked me, too."

And in that one sentence Michelle understood that not all of Tara's boyfriends had liked Brandon, and even at a young age he'd been insightful enough to realize it.

"Then one night Mom came home and said it was time to pack. Just like that. *It's time to pack, B.* That's what she called me. And she told me to pack like it was no big deal, no surprise. She told me that she had a new boyfriend, and we were moving in with him. I told her no, I wouldn't. Me and Johnson would be fine without her, she could just go. But I was little and she didn't listen. She made me move in with her and…I think it was Raphael. After that, I didn't like any of her guys too much, even the nice ones, 'cause I knew sooner or later, we'd leave them, too."

"Oh, Bran." Michelle had known her sister was flighty and moved around. All those years, she hadn't known Tara had a son she was dragging around after her. Thinking of Bran, so little and helpless, so lost, it hurt her…it was a physical pain.

"It's okay, Aunt Shell. I've got you now, and I know I'll never need to leave this house. Even if you're mad at me, like right now, you'll still try to do what's right. 'Cause you'll always take care of me. But, Aunt Shell, I want to know if this guy's my dad. I know you're worried that I'll find out my dad's not a good guy, but I know about guys that aren't good. And I know about guys who are like Johnson was. Neither of us know this Mr. McLean. We don't know if he's a good guy or not. Either way, I have to find out if he's my father. I love you, and I don't want to hurt you, but I'm going to get to know this guy. I'll figure out what kind he is. I'm pretty good at it."

There was a look of determination in his eyes, a maturity far beyond his years. It was a look that said she could try and keep him from Daniel, but he'd do whatever he needed to in order to spend time with this man.

"Can you give me a day or two to process all this? I mean, you've obviously been thinking about it, and planning this for some time. I just found Mr. McLean on my front porch, with no warning. So, let me think, and then you and I will figure something out."

"You promise?"

She nodded.

"Okay, then I promise I won't call him or go see him for two days."

Two days. She had two days to figure out what was best.

"Aunt Shell, I love you. I'm sorry I snuck around, but I had to know. You can punish me all you want."

Punishing him wasn't her first thought. Protecting him was. "I'm sorry I didn't listen and made you think you had to sneak around. I'll try and do better."

"Aunt Shell." Brandon ran over and threw his arms around her, something he rarely did anymore, now that he was too old for it to be cool. He clung to her a minute and said, "I love you."

She held on tight. "I love you, too, Bran. And somehow, I'll make this work out."

"He seemed okay, Aunt Shell. Even if he's not, I need to know that, too."

"Two days. Give me two days." She'd start by calling Henry Rizzo. Then she'd check on Daniel McLean. She took the card out of her pocket. McLean's Restoration. He said that he was doing some work for Christopher Brothers Construction. She'd start there.

IT WAS THREE O'CLOCK in the morning and Daniel was still awake.

He'd come home from Brandon and Michelle's house and

paced for an hour, then, needing something to do, he'd gone out back to split wood.

Piece after piece, he had slammed the maul into the wood. Despite the cold, he'd worked up a sweat. His arms had started to burn every time he raised the maul, but he didn't stop. He pushed himself, releasing the red heat of his anger on the wood.

It was pitch-black by the time he went back inside.

His golden retriever, Chloe, who'd made herself decidedly absent, crawled out from under the table. She seemed to sense that his anger was fading, and that Daniel was now just hurting. Hurting at the idea of a world without Tara and her boundless optimism in it. Hurting at the thought of a son he'd never known about.

Hurting.

Daniel hadn't felt so much pain since his grandparents had died. They'd given him such a normal, happy childhood. Something his own parents hadn't been able, or willing, to do. He still missed his grandparents in a way he'd never miss his mother or father.

He wished his grandfather was here, telling him what to do.

What was the right thing?

Somewhere around midnight his anger toward Tara had dulled from acute pain to a constant throbbing. That's when he finally started mourning his old friend. Whenever he thought of Tara the word *flitter* came to mind. It's what she did during the time he'd known her. She'd flittered from one boyfriend to another, rather like she moved from one table to another in the restaurant. She preached following your dreams and finding happiness. So he'd started McLean's Restoration. Still, he was grateful for his grandfather encouraging him to complete a business degree. It had proved invaluable to him.

Chloe jumped onto the couch, and sat as close to him as she could without actually being on top of him. He ran his hand through the dog's thick coat garnering some comfort from the contact. She sighed and plopped her head on his thigh.

It was hard to imagine Tara not telling him he was a father.

But they'd had that one night and there was a chance he was Daniel's father. Tara had broken up with her last boy-friend—for the life of him, Daniel couldn't think of the man's name—a few weeks, maybe a month and a half before they shared their one night together, if he was remembering correctly. But he had no idea what she'd done afterward, who she'd moved on to.

Brandon had looked so scared yet so proud when Daniel had opened the door and found him on the porch.

And Brandon's aunt, Michelle, had looked so hurt and ter-rified.

The whole situation was a mess.

How could Tara have a son and never tell the boy, or her own sister, who the father was? What kind of person did that?

A person who was so concerned with chasing her own dreams and happiness that she could ignore everyone else's feelings.

He'd always thought of her in such warm, glowing terms, even after she'd left him without a word. Tara had been a free spirit. But now, he saw that her idea of freedom was selfish. It hadn't taken anyone else into consideration and it had left a trail of pain in her wake.

When Michelle had said how her sister had never even told her that she had a son, he'd seen the pain and understood just how selfish Tara had been.

He wished she was here so he could tell her how much she'd hurt all three of them. But she was gone, and there was no going back. All they could do was pick up the pieces and move on as best they could.

All he could do was try to find a way to do that without causing anyone any more stress.

Chapter Three

Michelle's two-day grace period went too fast.

She'd arranged for Daniel to meet her at a small coffee-house, Monarch's, on Perry Square during her lunch break. She arrived ten minutes early, snagged a table in the back corner and waited nervously for him to arrive. She tried to pull herself together, but was afraid she wasn't doing a very good job of it. She'd felt as if she were one hiccup away from a full-blown panic attack since Daniel McLean had introduced himself.

He walked into the restaurant and stood just inside the doorway, scanning the room, allowing her a moment to study him. When he'd shown up on her doorstep on Tuesday, she'd been too floored to really look at the man. His hair was brown. But the color didn't go quite far enough. There was a slight hint of auburn in it as the rare December sunshine streamed through the window onto it. He was tall, somewhere just over six feet, she imagined. He smiled as he spotted her and headed to her table.

Michelle felt a surge of panic as he approached. She didn't want to do this. She didn't want this stranger disrupting the life she'd built with her nephew.

Daniel reached her table and said, "I wasn't sure you'd be here."

"I told you I would be." She didn't admit how much she'd like to be anywhere but here.

He took off his coat, threw it to the end of the bench and slid into the booth. "But that didn't mean you would."

"I'm realistic enough to admit I don't have a choice. I can't run away from this problem." No matter how much she'd like to.

"Problem," he echoed.

"Sorry, poor choice of words."

A perky blond waitress with a ready smile came up to the table, a pot of coffee in her hand. "I thought I'd see if your friend wanted anything, and whether or not you were ready for something to go with your coffee?"

"I'll take a coffee," Daniel said, tossing the waitress a careless smile.

Michelle watched the girl blush as she poured Daniel's coffee. She seemed to forget Michelle was even at the table. "My coffee could use warming," she said to remind her.

The girl looked flustered and the rosy glow in her cheeks intensified. "Sorry." She topped off Michelle's coffee. "You two just holler then if you want something else."

"Where were we?" Daniel took a sip of his coffee, oblivious to the fact the waitress was still glancing back at him. "Oh, *problem.* You were saying that you can't run from this problem. It was an honest choice of words, I guess. Neither of us expected this or went looking for this, but here we are, and neither of us can run from it. So, what are we going to do?"

"We could wait until Brandon is eighteen, and he could decide whether or not he wants the paternity test then," she said. "Not going to happen, is it? Neither of you would wait five years, would you?"

"No. I think you know that."

Michelle nodded. "I do, but I had to ask. And even if you agreed, Brandon wouldn't."

"So, what have you decided? Where do you want to go from here?"

"I called your friend Josh, and he assured me you were the best. Not only a good worker, but a good friend." He'd also told her how he'd met Daniel. A subcontractor had left him high and dry, and he'd called Daniel, a man he didn't know, asking for help. Daniel was already committed to a project, but had come in nights for two weeks straight to help. *He's that guy, the one who would bend over backward to help out a stranger. The one his friends can always count on, and rarely, if ever, asks for anything for himself.*

The fact that he was *that guy* didn't make Michelle feel better. It made her feel worse, because if Daniel had been something else, someone else, she might have had an excuse to try to prevent him from finding out if he was Brandon's father.

"I talked to an attorney, a dad from Erie Elementary. He agreed that the first thing we'd want to do is the test. We'd have to wait a couple weeks for the results." First, she'd had two days to figure out what to do, and now, in just weeks, her whole life could be turned upside down.

"And if I am Brandon's father?"

Michelle studied the man sitting across from her. If she'd met him at a party, she might have been attracted to him. But given the circumstances, she couldn't afford to be. She looked for some of Brandon in him. There was just the slightest hint that his hair could have been the same rusty shade as Brandon's when he was younger. They both had the same warm, brown eyes. But Tara's eyes had been brown, as well. And if she remembered her high school biology class, brown was a dominant gene, blue recessive. So even if Brandon's father's eyes had been blue, Brandon could still have Tara's brown eyes.

"You're staring," Daniel said.

"Oh. Sorry. Of course, you must be used to it."

"No."

"Oh, come on, the waitress is still checking you out every chance she can sneak a peek. Not that I was looking at you like her. I mean…" She was digging a hole. "I was looking for some of Brandon in you, or you in him."

"And did you find it?"

She shrugged. "I don't know."

"You didn't answer my question. If I am Brandon's father, then what?"

"Let's just start with finding out if you are. I hope you don't think I'm presumptuous, but I made an appointment for you tonight, if you can make that. I'm taking Brandon in the morning before school." She passed him a Post-it with the doctor's office information and time.

Daniel took the paper. "I'll find a way to make it work."

Michelle started to gather her coat and purse, but Daniel continued, "Now about me seeing Brandon."

She set her coat back down. "I don't think that's wise until after we get the results."

"Is he willing to wait?" Daniel asked softly.

Michelle didn't answer, because Brandon had made it clear he wasn't.

"I take that as he's not."

"I'm not comfortable with the idea of a total stranger having unrestricted access to my nephew."

"So restrict it. You be there, too. Maybe we could start by you two coming to my house on Saturday for lunch. I'll cook, and give you a tour of the house and my shop. You can meet Chloe, as well. I think Brandon will love her, and I can guarantee that she'll love him."

"Mr. McLean, I'm not ready for Brandon to hang around with you. What makes you think I'd want him socializing with your girlfriend?"

"Ah, I'm back to being Mr. McLean in that schoolmarmish tone of yours." He tsked. "Chloe's my dog, if that matters."

"Dog?"

"Chloe's a golden retriever. She loves kids."

"Oh."

"It's only lunch, Michelle. And you'll be there. I'm pretty sure that Brandon's pestering you."

Despite herself, Michelle laughed. "He's a pit bull. He won't let up." She'd gotten her two days to make a decision, but with the way Brandon had continually harped, asking if she'd made a decision, wanting to call Daniel, there'd been very little reprieve.

"Then I'll keep this appointment tonight, and let's try Saturday and see how it works," Daniel coaxed. "We can decide where we go after that."

"Mr. McLean—"

"Daniel," he corrected.

"I know you didn't come looking for this, but—"

"Can you imagine what it's like finding out you might have a kid? A kid who's thirteen? One you never knew anything about?"

"No. Maybe not, but I do know what it's like to have your sister show up on your doorstep with an eight-year-old, a nephew you never knew anything about. I know what it's like to have her say she was dying. I know what it's like to be twenty-four, starting a new job and trying to deal with hospice and a grieving little boy who was for all intents and purposes a stranger."

"Sorry," he said softly. "That was rough."

"I'm sorry, too."

"Michelle, even if Brandon's not mine, he's Tara's. And despite how she left, she was a good friend. I'd like to get to know her son…and her sister. So Saturday?"

Michelle wished she could say no, but she could see how much Daniel wanted this, and she knew Brandon would, as well. It would be fine. She'd be there.

She nodded. "Okay then. I realize you and Brandon didn't actually spend much time together on Tuesday. So, yes. We'll have lunch at your house, but I'm not promising anything beyond that."

"For now, I'll take it."

"That's good because, for now, it's all that I can give you."

The waitress came back. "Anything else, folks?"

"No, we were just finishing," Michelle said.

The young woman tore off their bill and set it on the table. Daniel had money on top of it before Michelle could even reach for her purse.

"I've got it," he said.

"Fine. But next time, it's on me."

"Deal." He smiled and walked her to the door. "We can make this work, Michelle. I swear, no matter what, the two of us will make this work for Brandon. I know what it's like to be a kid and feel abandoned by your parents. I would never do that to a kid. Never."

There was a vehemence in his words. Michelle knew he meant them wholeheartedly. And for the life of her, she couldn't decide if that was a comfort or not.

THE NEXT DAY was the first Friday in December. Just a few weeks until Christmas.

Just a few weeks until the Christmas Fair.

Normally, the fair would be foremost on Michelle's mind. She would be all aflutter with plans and a large to-do list. But given the circumstances, the fair was way down on her list as Michelle walked into Erie Elementary's meeting room and found Carly, habitually late Carly, already there. "You're never going to believe what happened to me," she said in unison with her friend.

Neither of them even attempted to laugh at the fact they'd both said the same thing at the same time as a greeting.

"It seems like we've been starting every meeting this way. You want to start?" Michelle asked as she shed her coat and hat and placed them on the couch before joining Carly at the table.

"Might as well wait for Samantha," Carly answered. "That way I don't have to tell the story twice."

"Fine."

They sat in a very comfortable silence and didn't have to wait long until Samantha walked in. Her very demeanor practically radiated happiness.

"Hi," she sang out. "You two will never guess what happened."

"That's just what I said to Michelle when she came in." Carly sounded even more depressed.

"And I said it back to her," Michelle echoed. "Neither of you are going to believe my holiday."

Samantha got settled, and set a box of pumpkin squares in the center of the table. "Talking about the Christmas Fair can wait a minute. Sounds like there's a lot going on, so who goes first? Alphabetical order?"

"Good news first," Carly said. "And by the look of things, Samantha, you're the only one with that, so you go."

Michelle nodded in agreement. She'd live vicariously through Samantha's happiness for a few minutes. She suspected that it had something to do with Erie Elementary's interim principal.

"Come on, Samantha," Carly prompted.

As if she couldn't contain her news another second, Samantha practically shouted out, "I'm in love."

"That's not news," Michelle and Carly said in unison. They looked at each other and this time they did laugh.

"Really, it was that obvious?" Samantha asked.

Carly snorted a response.

Samantha laughed again. "I wish one of you had clued me in because it was news to me. And even more important, Harry loves me back."

"No news there, either," Michelle told her. "Anyone looking at the two of you at the Thanksgiving Pageant knew that. But is he making the principal's job permanent?"

"We selfishly don't want to lose you," Carly assured her.

"He is. He talked to the superintendent and he'll be staying on at Erie Elementary as the new principal. We're going to take it slow. We don't want to make any mistakes, but I don't think anything about what Harry and I have could be a mistake. We fit. Now, Michelle, your turn," Samantha said.

Michelle hadn't realized how much she'd been counting on their support until this minute, as she said, "Remember when I said Brandon wanted to find his father?"

"And he agreed to wait until he was eighteen," Samantha said.

"Well, he lied. He went looking anyway, and he found him—maybe. I don't know what I'm going to do."

"Oh, Michelle." Samantha's voice was full of sympathy. She pulled Michelle to her and enveloped her in a hug, much as she might have done for one of her kids.

Carly, who didn't do any kind of emotional display with the

ease that Samantha did, didn't say anything but she took Michelle's hand and squeezed it.

Feeling not only comforted but bolstered, Michelle went on. "All I can do right now is wait and see what happens when the results of the paternity test are in. So, I'm not worrying." She wanted to tell them how afraid she was. She wanted to confess that she hated change, but this was something so foreign, so scary, that she hadn't managed a full night's sleep since Daniel McLean had shown up on her doorstep. "I can't talk about it any more right now. Carly?"

Samantha smiled and turned to Carly, as well. "Carly? Your turn."

Carly sighed. "I spent Friday at the police station."

Michelle had known that something was really wrong with Carly. She had been having problems with her ex all fall. But this?

"You can't just leave it there," Samantha coaxed.

Michelle felt a pang of guilt for not doing more for Carly sooner. "What happened?"

"Well, remember when I told you about redecorating my ex's office?"

"And finding him on the couch that you bought," Michelle replied. Tough, indomitable Carly had tried to put on a brave front, but Michelle had seen how recalling the incident, even now, tore at her.

"And not just him. No, I saw Dean *and* his secretary. I mean, having an affair with a secretary. How cliché."

"Things wouldn't become a cliché if they didn't happen often in real life," Samantha said softly.

"Well, with the mediator we worked out the whole settlement except for that couch. I spent months shopping for the perfect one, and I deserved to keep it. I'll confess, I might have been a bit obsessed. But I fought for that couch, even though Dean wanted it." Carly took a deep, cleansing breath. "Long story short, I won. He brought that stupid couch over the day after Thanksgiving when he brought the kids home. Getting that couch, well, it was like a milestone, really marking the end of our marriage. And I wanted nothing more than to be finished with it. I wanted to be more like Samantha when she went through her divorce and let all the anger and recriminations go. I needed to put the past behind me and move on to the next chapter of my life."

"I don't think I follow how that led to you spending time in jail," Samantha said slowly.

Michelle was grateful Samantha said it, because she didn't understand, either.

"You see, I had Sean and his dad carry it into the backyard. They set it next to the shed. And I went into the shed, grabbed the gas can and, while Dean watched, I doused the couch and lit it on fire."

"You burned the couch, after fighting so hard for it?" Michelle asked.

"Come on. Really. Would you ever have been able to sit on it? Or even look at it and not remember what you'd seen happening on it? I'm not just talking about him having sex with another woman. When I saw the two of them, I saw my whole life—years of what I thought was a happy marriage—go up in smoke. I wanted to purge myself of that memory. I want to move on to a happier, better future."

"So you burned it," Michelle added.

Carly nodded, looking chagrined. "So I burned it. Fire's supposed to be cleansing."

"And that's illegal?" Samantha asked.

"Well, probably. But I don't think I would have got in too

much trouble for simply burning a couch…if the shed hadn't caught on fire, too."

"Oh, no," Samantha and Michelle both said.

"To make matters worse, the neighbor's shed, which is right next to mine, caught, as well."

"Oh" was all Michelle could think of to say.

"And finally, the kicker was when the fire department came, and the police right along with them."

"And you spent a night in jail?" Samantha asked.

"No. This very annoying lieutenant was the first to arrive. He said he didn't go on many calls, but he was close so he stopped in to check on things. We didn't quite see eye to eye, Lieutenant Jefferson and I. He'd have probably kept me overnight, if it had been up to him. But then this cute patrolman showed up and took over. I had to go down to the station and answer some questions. Officer Kent charged me with a criminal mischief misdemeanor, then I got to go home."

"So what happens now?"

"I have a hearing, but Henry Rizzo is representing me. He talked to the ADA and they worked out a deal. The hearing is just a formality. I'll have to pay restitution to my neighbor, which I've already done, and as long as I don't burn down anything else in the neighborhood for a year, my record will be expunged." She sighed. "It was stupid, but it's over. Maybe we should talk about the Christmas Fair now."

Michelle could sense that Carly had needed to unburden as much as she had, but there was only so much unburdening a person could take all at once, so she pulled the file from her bag. "Well, I know what they did last year, and the PTA has given me some money to shop with. So I think we're on track. The eighth-graders need community service hours and a few teachers are having them make a number of the crafts. There was a note from the previous coordinator that some of the games need fixing, and…" She shrugged.

Normally, knowing she was in charge of an event like this would have had her fretting, checking and rechecking her lists. Frankly, she couldn't muster that kind of concern today. "It's all good."

"What do you need us to do?" Samantha asked.

"I need you to concentrate on your new boyfriend, and Carly, I need you to concentrate on this hearing. I've got this under control."

"What about Brandon's possible father?"

"Brandon and I are having lunch with him on Saturday."

"Why don't you ask him to help with the Christmas Fair? He's a guy. He could help with the lifting and whatever other manly things need doing."

"He is some kind of carpenter. I suppose he'd be able to repair the games that need it. And I'd be there the whole time." She looked at Samantha. "Is that what you'd do? I mean, you've managed to let Phillip back into the kids' lives so gracefully. What do you think?"

"I think if Brandon wants to spend time with this man, it would be better if he did it with you there, if he felt you were on his side. You have to believe it will all work out for the best. Look at Harry and me. Despite our hurdles, I've never been so happy."

"Yeah, I just have to believe." Michelle wished she could be as optimistic as Samantha, but she couldn't seem to believe in the idea that this would work out. "So maybe I'll ask him."

They wrapped up the meeting and all three walked out together. "Listen, don't wait until the next meeting. If you need us, call," Samantha said.

"Yeah. If this guy gives you any trouble, I'll take care of him.

I've already got a record, what more can they do to me?" Carly was joking, and she laughed as she said the words, but Michelle could see that their friend was really worried about the hearing.

She reached out and took Carly's hand. "The same goes to you, too. You call if you need us. Do you need character witnesses at this hearing?"

Carly shook her head. "No. Henry says it's open and shut."

"Well, both of you just call me if you need me," Samantha said again as she hurried down the hall to where the principal's office light was still burning.

Michelle and Carly left together. "See you in two weeks," she said.

"See you then."

Michelle got in her car and drove home. She felt better than she had in days. She'd try to be as gracious as Samantha when dealing with Daniel, but she'd guard her nephew with Carly's ferocity. And in the end, she knew if she needed them, she had friends who would be there for her.

There was comfort in that.

Chapter Four

On Saturday, Michelle tried to stick to her routine, because Brandon needed some sense of stability, in her opinion.

Unfortunately, in his opinion, he needed it to be eleven o'clock so they could head to Daniel's house.

"Can we leave a little early?" was his refrain, as they dusted, vacuumed and Michelle worked on the laundry. She had always used Saturday mornings for home maintenance, and had kept the tradition alive even after Brandon came to live with her. "No. We have chores to do before we leave, and Mr. McLean isn't expecting us until a little after eleven."

Somehow they made it to the designated time. Brandon had heard the grandmother clock chime and had grabbed the car keys along with his coat. "Come on, Aunt Shell."

Michelle moved a little slower. She slipped on her coat and caught herself checking her reflection in the mirror. "This isn't a date," she scolded herself sternly, then realized how stupid she must have sounded. She was thankful no one had been around to hear her. She took her purse off the hook and locked the door behind her as she went out to the car.

Brandon didn't seem happy that she wasn't sprinting to the car, so he leaned over and beeped the horn.

She gave him *the look*. It was a mother's look, even though she was only an aunt. A look that said *that's enough, I mean it*. She didn't have to use that look often with Brandon, but it was probably better to let him know where they stood now, rather than wait until they were at Daniel's house.

She should have invited Daniel to lunch at her house. That way she'd have given herself the home-field advantage. But it was too late to try to switch today's location. Anyway, this wasn't a war. She didn't need an upper hand. What she needed was enough wisdom to keep Brandon from being hurt.

Brandon was quiet until they reached the street, off Wattsburg Road, that led to Daniel's house. "There, Aunt Shell. Turn left there."

She obliged. They drove maybe a mile down the road, before she spotted the first house. It sat back from the street, nestled in amongst the trees, looking for all intents and purposes as if it had grown there.

It was a small, one-story building—a cottage more than a house. There was a door in the center of the building, and two windows closely spaced on either side. But what really drew her to the house was the huge front porch that spanned the entire width of it. There were four wooden rocking chairs on it, two on either side of the door. Each pair had a wooden table between them.

The porch's railings were woven with evergreen boughs and there was a huge evergreen wreath, tied with a red bow, on the front door.

"That's it," Brandon shouted, just in case Michelle hadn't realized it.

She pulled into the driveway, and caught a glimpse of a barn back behind the house. Brandon reached for the door handle.

"Hold on one minute. I need to remind you that, no matter

what, I love you. I need you to listen to me, and trust that anything I tell you is for your own good. Can you remember that?" She wanted him to understand that she was in control.

"Sure," he said. "Can I go in now?"

Michelle sighed. "Yes. Be polite and remember what I said."

"I will. You're the boss and I'm polite." And with that, he bolted from the car and ran to the front door, which flew open before he even had a chance to knock.

Michelle walked at a much more sedate pace than Brandon. Daniel stepped out onto the porch. He was wearing a soft-looking blue-and-green flannel shirt over a plain navy T-shirt, and a pair of well-worn jeans. There was a huge golden retriever next to him. "Hi."

"Hi," Michelle echoed, not sure what else to say.

Brandon stepped into the house, the dog following him. He knelt on the floor, petting her, while she licked his face as if greeting an old friend. Michelle entered, as well.

"I'm glad you came." Daniel shut the door behind them. "That's Chloe," Daniel told her.

Chloe, hearing her name, pricked up her ears and, after giving Brandon another huge lick, came over to Michelle and sat, with an almost audible plop, down in front of her.

"She's waiting for you to say hi," Daniel explained.

"Just pat her head and tell her she's pretty," Brandon added. He looked at Daniel. "She's not real good with animals."

Michelle had never had a dog. She'd had friends with dogs, but she was uncomfortable around them. Brandon was watching her expectantly, though, so putting her discomfort aside, she leaned over and awkwardly patted the big dog's head. "Nice girl."

Brandon just shook his head, and Michelle knew she'd flunked the greeting-dogs test in her nephew's eyes.

Daniel, however, smiled. "Come on in. Would you like a tour before lunch?"

Before Michelle could politely tell him that wasn't necessary, Brandon jumped to his feet and yelled, "Yeah. I didn't get to see inside last time." His noise sent Chloe trotting back over to him for a more satisfying pat. Brandon enthusiastically obliged and petted the dog.

Michelle was about to warn him that maybe he was being too rough when Daniel said, "Oh, she likes that. You're going to have a friend for life, Brandon." He turned to Michelle. "Okay, the tour. This is the living room, not to state the obvious or anything. I've done all the renovating myself. I pulled up a lovely orange shag carpet and found the hardwood floor. I refinished it, and then moved on to…" He paused. "I'll spare you the details, but suffice to say, this house looks nothing like when I bought it."

He was proud. Deservedly so, Michelle admitted as he took them through the small cottage, room to room. The house was beautiful. And bigger than she'd thought it would be from the outside. There were three generous bedrooms, only one of which, Daniel's, was habitable. "I'll get to the other two after I've finished the public sections of the house," he told her.

He wrapped up the tour in the kitchen, which was the subject of his current project. He was hand carving a beautiful mantelpiece for the fireplace. He'd set up a makeshift workstation in one corner. But the room was sufficiently finished for Michelle to see what it would be.

"It's going to be beautiful," she assured him.

"Have a seat. I just made soup and have to get the sandwich stuff out." Chloe left Brandon's side, walked to the back door and sat down. "Oh, Clo wants out."

"Can I take her outside?" Brandon asked.

"Sure," Daniel started, then glanced at Michelle. "If your aunt doesn't mind."

"Sure," she agreed, wishing she could think of a reason to say no. Things felt stilted between her and Daniel, even with Brandon in the room. She didn't want to think about how bad it would be between them without her nephew running interference. "You need a coat on, though."

Brandon didn't spare a second for complaints about how he didn't need a coat. He just grabbed it and was out the back door with Chloe before he even had it zipped.

DANIEL WATCHED Brandon bolt out the door with Chloe. He could see the two of them running around out in the backyard. "I wish I had that kind of energy," he jokingly said to Michelle, hoping to break the ice.

"Yes, I've often thought the same thing." That was it. She didn't offer up anything else.

Daniel didn't know what to say. Actually, he had so much he wanted to say he didn't know where to start. "Thanks for coming today. Really, I mean it."

"I know we don't know each other well, Mr. McLean, but when I say I'm going to do something, I make every effort to do it."

"Daniel, please."

She sighed and nodded. "It's easier to keep you at arm's length if you're Mr. McLean, but Daniel it is. You may call me Michelle."

He knew she didn't intend to sound cute, but her regal-like permission, so grudgingly given, was in fact cute. He didn't share the insight because he doubted she'd enjoy it. "I don't expect us to be best friends, Michelle, but I'd like to think we can be friendly. I'm not trying to hurt you or Brandon. I just want to get to know him."

"And I don't know you well enough to know if I can trust you with him. Part of me wants to be selfish, just this once. I want to tell you no. Back off. Leave us alone. The two of us have worked hard to get over Tara's death and my mother's indifference. We've built our own little family. And it works."

"Michelle, I get that. I do. But if he's my son? If Tara never told me, and Brandon's mine? I can't wait for the test results. Your doctor said the lab can take forever, especially this time of year."

"Yeah, holiday paternity testing. Who knew it was this year's hot Christmas item?" She shook her head. "Sorry, lame jokes are my forte when I'm nervous or upset."

"Which are you now?"

"Both," she admitted. "I didn't ask for this."

"Neither did I," he assured her.

"And yet, here we are, stuck with it. You know, all my life I've been the good girl. I watched Tara run amok, causing my parents so much pain. It got worse after my father died. Mom couldn't control her and eventually she stopped trying. And Tara never worried about anyone but herself. So, I worked hard not to rock the boat. I never broke curfew, did well at school, went to college. I tried to make up for Tara by being the perfect daughter. She used to call me *the good sister*. It wasn't a term of endearment, it was mocking. But I never had a chance to be anything but that."

He was surprised Michelle had shared that so readily. She didn't strike him as someone quite so open with her thoughts and feelings. "It must have been hard."

Michelle's words continued to spill over one another in their haste to break free. "It was. Maybe I wanted to sneak out to a party when I was younger. Maybe I wanted to do something wild and crazy. And maybe, just this once, I don't want to try to see the other side. I don't want to know you, Daniel McLean.

I don't want to hear about your pain, learning that you had a son so long after the fact. I don't want to listen, or be understanding. Maybe, just this once, I want to think about me. Not what's best for you or for Brandon. I just want you to go away and things to get back to normal." Michelle looked slightly horrified at her outburst.

"Feel better?" he asked.

She nodded. "I'm so sorry. That's not like me."

"I'm glad you said it all. Listen, Michelle, I'm sorry—truly sorry—that Tara put you, put us both, in this situation. You don't like it. I get that. But there it is. We're both going to have to figure out where to go from here. I know you'd like me to go away, but I can't."

Brandon and the dog burst into the kitchen. "Hey, Chloe catches balls real good—" He stopped and stared at Daniel. "I don't know what to call you. We don't know if you're my dad till we get the DNA test back."

"Why don't you just call me Daniel."

Brandon nodded. "That will do."

"Come on and sit down now. Daniel made us lunch," Michelle said.

Daniel hurried and got everything out. He wished Brandon had stayed out a bit longer. Maybe he could have explained things better to Michelle. But she did seem a bit more at ease despite—or maybe because of—her outburst. His soup was nothing special, but it was hearty and the three of them made short work of it and the sandwiches. He thought the chocolate–peanut butter dessert was festive, albeit just as simple. "Would you like to finish the grand McLean tour by walking out to my workshop?"

"Is it out in the barn?" Brandon asked, already pulling on his coat and heading for the back door with Chloe.

"He doesn't do anything by halves, does he?" Daniel asked Michelle as they retrieved their own coats.

"No, he doesn't."

He thought she was going to stop at that short sentence, but as they reached the back door, she said, "When Tara and Brandon showed up on my doorstep, he was already an old soul. He was only eight, but he got them both settled. And as much as I tried to shield him from the inevitability of her cancer, he knew. He took care of her, as much as an eight-year-old could. It wasn't until after she died that he asked, 'What's going to happen to me now?' There was such a sense of resignation in his voice. He'd spent his whole life moving whenever Tara took it in her head. I told him then and there that he'd always have a home with me. He's grown a bit younger since then, if that makes sense. But he's still got an old-soul quality to him. When he makes up his mind, he just steamrollers his way to his goal."

Daniel drank in the details and thought of Brandon's early years. Never knowing where home was. Following Tara's wanderlust. He didn't think that could have been easy on a young boy.

Brandon was throwing the ball for Chloe again, but as Daniel and Michelle reached the shop, both the boy and the dog came running.

Daniel flipped on the light switch as they entered.

"Daniel, this isn't what I thought a workshop would look like," Michelle said as she studied the space.

"What did you think?"

"Messy, tools everywhere. Sawdust and such. This is wonderful."

He'd taken the entire ground floor of the barn, about twice the space of his entire cottage, and transformed it. Tools hung from the walls, and whatever couldn't hang was neatly arranged on shelves. His big power tools sat in a cluster, and while they were necessary, it was the antique tools that he was most proud of. He had an electric heater, and also a woodstove for heat in the winter.

"See this?" He ran his hand lovingly over his newest piece. "It's a fully functional 1876 Schrofter Brothers jig."

Michelle smiled. "Brandon used to get just that look in his eyes when he got a new video game."

"You think we look the same, Aunt Shell?" he asked excitedly.

"I think you both definitely get that geeky glee sort of look in your eyes," she admitted.

Not for the first time, Daniel searched the boy's features for some sense of the familiar. Maybe Brandon had Grandpa's nose? And there was the tiniest bit of a dimple in his right cheek when he smiled, just like Daniel's grandmother used to have. Daniel wondered if what he thought he saw he really saw, or was it just wishful thinking?

Was he wishing Brandon was his? He wasn't sure. He hadn't given any thought to having kids until Brandon showed up on his doorstep and asked if he could be his son.

"It's all so cool." Brandon was standing by an antique secretary.

Daniel had bought the piece at a garage sale he happened to be driving by. It had only been ten dollars, which was a fair price given that pieces of glass were broken, and some of the ornate carving above the mirror had been broken off. "I've been working on it. When I'm done, you won't know it was ever damaged. See." He pointed at a piece of the molding. "I already fixed the center of this." It was seamlessly repaired.

"Where did you learn to do this?" Brandon took the piece and studied it.

"My grandfather dabbled in carpentry. He taught me."

Michelle was on the other side of the barn, looking at one of his scrapbooks with pictures of projects he'd either built or restored.

"You were lucky to have a grandpa. Do I have one?" Brandon asked, then hastily added, "If I'm your son, I mean. Mom and Aunt Shell's dad died, and their mom, my grandmother, lives in Texas, so I never see her."

Daniel wished he could lie to the boy, that he could tell him some fairy-tale story about the wonderful grandfather he'd get if Daniel was his father. "My dad left right after I was born, and though he was around for a while when I was really little, I don't remember him. My mom left when I was a bit bigger. She left me with my grandma and grandpa, and they're the ones who raised me."

"Oh, like me and Aunt Shell."

Daniel nodded. "Just like that. I always knew my grandparents loved me and would always be there for me, just like you know that about your aunt."

Brandon nodded. "Yeah. I knew she'd be mad I came and found you, but I knew she'd love me anyway."

"That's a gift," Daniel assured him. "Finding people who love you and are there for you, who you can count on, no matter what."

"Guess we were both lucky, huh?"

"Yeah, I guess we were." When Daniel was young he hadn't thought of living with his grandparents instead of his parents as being particularly lucky, but as he grew older, he learned to appreciate how fortunate he'd been. "And I've always promised myself that if I ever had kids, I'd be there for them. I'd be the kind of parent my grandparents were, not like my own mom and dad. Does that make sense?"

"Yeah."

"I just want you to know that you're lucky to have your aunt and know you can count on her. If I'm your dad, I hope you come to realize you can count on me that way, too." Brandon was smiling, and Daniel looked up to find Michelle had come back over and was studying him. "I'll try to never hurt either of you," he added for her benefit.

She seemed to understand what he was saying, and nodded. "The piece is beautiful," she said, studying the secretary.

"Daniel got it for only ten bucks at a garage sale. Can you believe it? He's fixing the broken glass and the broken pieces, and it's gonna be cool when he's all done with it. You'll never even know it had been broken."

"You're having a good time," she said.

"Oh, sure."

She didn't look happy or upset that Brandon was enjoying himself. She looked as if she were steeling herself for something. "Mr. McLean—Daniel—I know you and Brandon want to spend time together. And I had a thought."

"Yes?" he asked. He'd been worried that today was it. That she was going to make him wait for the results of the test before he spent more time with Brandon.

"Erie Elementary—"

"My school," Brandon interrupted.

"Yes, Brandon's school. It's having a Christmas Fair the Monday before Christmas."

"It's our last day of school before Christmas break," Brandon practically crowed with excitement. He paused and added, "Two weeks from Monday."

"What's a Christmas Fair, exactly?" Daniel asked.

"The school has kindergarten through eighth grade. The PTA provides gifts that the kids can buy for their family—"

"Last year I got Aunt Shell a necklace."

"Little things they can buy inexpensively," she continued. "Crafts people have made, small things the PTA has bought. The kids shop for their family's presents—"

Brandon interrupted again. "And there are games we can play and win prizes for ourselves."

"We have a small luncheon for all our PTA workers. And what money the fair makes goes into a fund to buy the items for next year," she finished.

"Okay, I get it. A place for the kids to shop and have a bit of fun while they're at it."

"Yes. Besides the games, there's a Chinese auction where the kids can win prizes and use them as gifts, as well—"

"Or we can keep 'em. Last year, I won a Mercyhurst Prep sweatshirt, and I tried to give it to Aunt Shell, but it didn't fit her, so I've got it."

Daniel laughed.

Michelle smiled and shot Brandon a look that radiated her love for the boy.

She didn't seem to realize how much of herself she'd shown him today, as she continued, "I'm in charge of the Christmas Fair this year, and I'd thought I'd have the other two school-mothers on the committee help me get ready, but they both have other things going on right now. Important, all-consuming sorts of things. So, I thought that maybe you could help me out, and I could let them off the hook. Brandon and I will be working on the fair every day between now and the twenty-second. It would mean fixing a few games, helping make a few crafts—"

"It doesn't matter what it means," Daniel assured her. He'd get to see them—Brandon, he corrected himself—he'd get to see Brandon every day. "I'm in. When do we start?"

"Monday after school? I don't know when you get off work,

but I've arranged my schedule so that I can be there around three each day for the next two weeks. I'd rather do an hour or two each day getting everything ready than a few killer days at the end."

"Aunt Shell likes being prepared. And the earlier she's ready, the better," Brandon told him, laughing in such a way that Daniel knew this was an inside joke between the two of them.

"I can juggle my schedule and be there at three for as long as you need me. That's the advantage of working for yourself."

"Fine. Then we'll see you Monday at three. But right now, we'd better be going. We need to stop at the grocery store on the way home."

"Aunt Shell—" Brandon started, then stopped when he saw her expression.

It wasn't mean or scary. She just lifted one eyebrow and crossed her arms over her chest and waited, watching him.

"Sure. You're right, we need to get other things done," Brandon agreed.

"And we really should let Mr. McLean—Daniel—get back to his own Saturday routine."

He'd tried the same kind of expression as she slipped and called him Mr. McLean. He was pleased to see that it worked as well for him because she'd immediately corrected herself and called him Daniel.

He'd like to argue that there was nothing he needed to do today. Nothing that was more important than spending time with them. He wanted to know more about Brandon, more about Michelle. But he didn't push. He sensed she was trying her best, and he appreciated it. So, he walked them out to the car.

"Do you know where Erie Elementary is?" she asked before she got into the car. He'd have thought Michelle would have some sedate-looking yuppie SUV. Black. Maybe gray. Instead she was driving a sporty orange sedan. It shouldn't have suited her, but it did.

"Daniel?"

"Oh, yes, I know where it is. I'll meet you there at three."

"Fine. We'll see you then. Thank you for lunch."

Brandon hadn't gotten into the car yet. Instead, he thrust out his hand. "Thank you for taking the afternoon off to spend with me, Daniel."

"You're welcome, Brandon. It was truly my pleasure."

Michelle backed her vehicle out of his driveway. Daniel patted Chloe and watched the car drive up the road and eventually out of sight.

He'd had fun. Something as simple as sharing a meal with Brandon and Michelle constituted the best time he'd had in recent memory.

"Come on, Clo." They started back into the house, but as he entered, it didn't give him the warm rush it usually did. Instead it felt cold and empty, because Brandon and Michelle had left.

Daniel didn't dwell on it as he sauntered through the house and out the back door toward his workshop.

He'd go to work on the secretary. He had an idea now what he'd do with it.

Chapter Five

Daniel had never been in Erie Elementary. He pulled up in front and parallel parked, then trudged through the slush-covered sidewalk into the entry hall, not quite sure where to go.

He'd spent yesterday supposedly working on the secretary in the workshop. He'd made so little progress that he was pretty sure it hardly qualified as working. His thoughts kept drifting to Brandon. Wondering if the boy was his son.

He tried to see his family—himself—in the boy, but all he managed to see was Brandon. There was no hint of the McLeans, no features that belonged to Tara, or even her sister, Michelle, at least not that he could see. In his eyes, Brandon Hamilton was wholly himself.

And that was saying a lot. For a thirteen-year-old boy, Brandon had a certain poise hidden beneath the gangly teen body. And a sense of purpose that Daniel admired.

Once Daniel had finished trying to categorize Brandon's features, to no avail, he started formulating questions. Things a father—or potential father—should know about his son.

What sports did he like?

What childhood illnesses had he suffered?

Broken bones?

What books did he read? Or did he even read for enjoyment? What were his dreams?

What did he want to be when he grew up?

On the heels of that question, Daniel realized that Brandon was in seventh grade.

That meant five years from now he'd be off to college. Which meant if Brandon was his son he only had a few years to make up for an entire lost childhood.

With that, he got angry at Tara all over again. How could she have denied him his son?

The same thoughts that had chased each other round and round yesterday, bringing his work to a standstill, left him standing still in the entryway as he replayed them.

"Can I help you?" asked a brunette with a ready smile.

"Sorry. I'm a bit lost." Which was a true statement if ever there was one. "I'm looking for Michelle Hamilton. I'm here to help with the Christmas Fair."

The woman gave him an assessing look. She grinned, as if whatever she'd seen she was pleased with. "You must be Daniel McLean."

He nodded. "Yes, I am."

Her smile grew even larger. "Well, it's nice to meet you, Daniel. I'm Samantha Williams. A good friend of Michelle's."

"Nice to meet you, too," he said.

"It's nice that you're willing to pitch in on the Christmas Fair." She chuckled. "That was a lot of nices. I'm not always so redundant."

He wasn't sure what to say next, so he played it safe and just smiled.

"Michelle says you know something about carpentry?"

"I own McLean Renovations, so it's what I do. Mainly detailed carpentry work. I just stripped and repaired a hundred-

and-fifty-year-old mantel from one of the mansions down by the courthouse. It was—" He stopped himself. He could go on and on about what he did, but he knew most people weren't interested.

"I'm afraid we won't have anything that challenging for you to do here."

"I don't know. A school full of kids?" As if on cue, two boys whizzed past them, running down the stairs.

"Walk," Samantha called out.

They slowed to a walk until they'd gone out the front door, then the two started racing over the slushy sidewalk, slipping and sliding all the way.

"Like I said." Daniel nodded toward the two boys who were rapidly disappearing from sight. "I'd say that working in a school is a bit more challenging than working in a quiet workshop with just the dog for company."

"Yes, learning to work with kids underfoot is a skill. Is it one you're hoping to acquire?" She was still smiling pleasantly, but her eyes narrowed as she studied him, waiting for his answer.

This *good friend* of Michelle's must know what was going on. This wasn't just a brief welcome to the school, it was an interrogation. At first it had been a subtle one, but with the last question, it had turned blatant.

"It appears there's a chance I'll need to," he answered, not exactly hedging, but if her frown was any indication, not being quite as forthright as she'd have preferred.

"Not my question. I asked if you were hoping to?" she pressed.

Daniel acknowledged that this woman had all the skills of a police interrogator. Seemingly, without effort, she'd found out what he did for a living, and now had somehow shifted to grilling him about whether he wanted Brandon to be his son.

He could tell her to back off, that it was none of her business, but he could see the concern in her face. Samantha Williams truly cared about Michelle and Brandon. How could he get annoyed about that?

"Listen, Ms. Williams, I'll be honest. This was as big a surprise for me as it was for Michelle. I haven't even begun to sort out my feelings. But I can assure you that if I need to acquire that particular skill, I will. I'm not the kind of man who'd walk away from my responsibilities."

She studied him a moment longer, then said, "I think you and I will get along well, Mr. McLean."

"Daniel," he told her, extending a hand.

"Daniel. And I'm Samantha." She shook his hand.

"Hey, Sami," a male voice called out from the top of the stairway. "What's taking so long?"

She smiled up at the man who was wearing a very loud Santa Claus tie. "And the bellowing man at the top of the stairs is Harry Remington, Erie Elementary's new principal."

"I'm not that new," the man complained affably as he walked down the stairs and joined them. "I've been here since September."

"Ah, but you were only the interim principal until recently, so I didn't count those first few months," Samantha assured him in a teasing tone.

Harry wrapped an arm around Samantha in such a way that Daniel realized they were a couple.

"Harry, this is Michelle's…uh, helper. Daniel McLean. Daniel, Harry."

"Oh, Daniel. I heard all about—" The man stopped short as Samantha gave him a slight jab of her elbow. "Oh, yes, well, I heard that you might be coming to help out with the Christmas Fair. Nice of you to spend some time with us." It was a good attempt at covering the fact that Harry knew about what was going on, as well. "We're always looking for volunteers."

"I'd like to get started. I'll need those directions to Michelle."

"She's in the basement storeroom," Samantha told him. "I was just heading downstairs and would be happy to show you."

"Thanks." Daniel turned to the principal. "Nice to meet you."

"Same here. Sami, hurry back up when you're done," Harry said, and turned to go back up the stairs.

Samantha started down the other flight and Daniel followed.

"So, Daniel," Samantha began to say as they reached the basement. "On behalf of everyone who knows and cares about Michelle and Brandon, I'd like to simply say, tread lightly. We don't want to see either of them hurt."

Daniel noted that although Samantha had all the finesse of a Mafia henchman, she had a loyalty that was admirable. "This isn't something I set out to do to your friend. I only want to do what's right for everyone."

"I guess that has to be enough. So, now, let's put you to work." She led him down a long hallway. "The basement has our kindergarten and preschool in it, as well as a few big storage rooms. One of them has all the PTA things."

The door was opened to the room she'd indicated. Daniel looked in the huge space that was lined with rows of stacked boxes and pieces of wood. There was a giant garbage can full of small rubber balls, garbage bags, sticks. The room seemed to be a jumble that made no discernible sense as he stood there taking it all in.

The one thing that was missing was any sign of Michelle.

"Hey, Michelle," Samantha hollered.

"I'm back here," she said, from way behind the mountain of boxes and bags.

"Don't come out," Samantha called. "I just wanted to be sure you were in here. I've brought Daniel down to assist you."

"Oh, Daniel's here?" Michelle popped out from the small path between the boxes and spotted him. "Great."

But it wasn't exactly excitement in her voice.

WHEN BRANDON FIRST CAME to live with her, a small part of Michelle had wanted someone—anyone—to take the responsibility out of her hands. Now, selfishness was back and it was wishing that Daniel McLean wasn't Brandon's father—that things could go back to the way they'd been and that Daniel would disappear from their lives. She felt guilty for harboring the longing, knowing how much Brandon wanted to have a father. From everything she could gather, Daniel was a nice enough man. And that was saying something, considering Tara's track record.

"You two have fun." Samantha grinned as she mouthed, *Yummy,* in Michelle's direction before she hurried out.

Oh, yeah, that's just what she needed, Samantha playing matchmaker. Of all the men in the universe that Michelle shouldn't be attracted to, Daniel had to be at the top of the list. Things were complicated enough.

Not that he wasn't attractive, but Michelle was planning to do her best to ignore that particular fact. Yes, she'd simply not notice that he was tall, that his hair always had a slightly mussed look that made her want to run her hand over it and smooth it and that his eyes danced when he smiled.

Yes, she'd ignore all that. Things had to stay strictly businesslike between them. If Daniel wasn't Brandon's father, he'd be leaving, and if he was, he'd be staying. Either way, she needed to keep him at a distance and do her best to protect Brandon, no matter which way it went.

"So where do you want me to start?" Daniel eyed the storage area.

"We have a Santa beanbag toss that has seen better days. Do you think you could take a look at it?"

"You're going to have to point the way. This place is a bit of a maze."

Despite her resolution to be all business, Michelle laughed. "When Samantha, Carly and I were assigned the Social Planning Committee, we thought we got the least popular PTA jobs there are. But if they ever institute a Storage Organizing Committee, that will be worse. Much worse."

"You can say that again," Daniel agreed readily. "What sort of social events is your committee responsible for?"

"Samantha just finished spearheading the Thanksgiving Pageant. It was quite the success, especially since it netted her a new boyfriend." Calling Harry Samantha's boyfriend didn't seem like a weighty enough description of what he was to her friend. She couldn't help feeling a bit of envy when she saw the two of them together. Someday, she wanted a relationship like that. Once she'd thought she was headed for something similar, but in the end it wasn't even close.

Where was she? Oh, the committee. "I'm in charge of the Christmas Fair, as you know. And Carly, our third member, is in charge of the Valentine's Dance. There's one more activity in the spring, but Heidi, the PTA president, is going to take care of that this year because she couldn't find any other volunteers."

"Oh. Sounds like…well, I was going to say fun, but really, it just sounds like work. A lot of work."

"Well, if I get it organized properly, it shouldn't be too bad, and the kids will have fun, and that's what's important."

"Speaking of kids, where's Brandon?"

"Oh, he'll be down soon. He's helping Mrs. Baker clean her

animal cages. She's the science teacher and had a lot of animals. He loves helping out."

"Does he have any pets? I've got a list of things I'd like to know about him. Things I should know if I'm—"

Michelle suspected he'd stopped short because of her. She'd felt herself start to frown. A list. He had a list of things he wanted to know about his possible son.

She tried to school her expression. His list of questions was a good thing. If he was interested enough to worry about knowing Brandon better, it was a good sign. "No, Bran doesn't have any pets. I work all day, so there's never been a good time to train a new animal. But he wants a dog desperately."

"Maybe for Christmas?"

"Probably not." She'd love to indulge Brandon and get him a dog, but she didn't think it was fair to leave one alone at home every day. She shouldn't feel as if she needed to justify her decision to Daniel.

He didn't argue, though he looked as if he'd like to. "Why don't you show me this beanbag toss."

Michelle led him to the corner where she'd been when they'd come into the room. "It's in there, toward the back, I think."

"And the rest?"

She shrugged. "I've got to confess, I don't know half of what's in here. Each year's PTA adds something. There's probably two decades' worth of paraphernalia."

"Okay, so why don't you start by telling me precisely how you run the Christmas Fair. What's included. I'll know what to keep my eyes out for as I search."

"Let's see, we hold it in the school gym. There are games the kids can pay to play, with prizes given out. We need an area for a Chinese auction."

"Chinese auction?"

She nodded. "A mainstay of any school activity. We ask local businesses for donations, and the kids buy tickets and drop their tickets into cans for the items to take a chance on items they want to win."

"What kind of things do you auction off?" he asked.

"Pretty much anything. There are toys, school gear, dinners at local restaurants."

"And you're in charge of this whole thing?" He shook his head. "I deal with deadlines and projects all the time, but I'll confess, this one would do me in. I might not have a clue what to do, but I follow instructions well, so you just tell me where to start."

"Beanbag toss."

"Okay. Let's go."

Michelle spotted a Santa hat at the top of a pile. "There."

Daniel nodded and started clearing boxes out to get to the game.

Michelle hurriedly returned to the door. She'd left her checklist there. She wanted to be sure they located everything today.

"Aunt Shell, is he here?" Brandon cried as he almost ran into her at full speed.

"Yes. He's in the back."

A look of palpable relief spread over Brandon's face.

She followed him as he sprinted to where Daniel was working.

The big man had already climbed back out with the Santa beanbag toss. It was almost Brandon's second collision.

"Bran, slow down," she hollered.

Brandon stopped in his tracks and Daniel peeked around the large plywood Santa. "Hi, Brandon."

"You came." Brandon was all smiles.

"I try to keep my promises, Brandon," he said gently.

In that moment, Michelle could almost believe his earnest expression. She could almost let herself believe that this man wouldn't hurt them, and that he'd be a good father to Brandon. Part of her would love to be that optimistic, trusting this person who seemed so nice, so honorable, so caring. But she couldn't afford to. She couldn't afford to let down her guard and risk this man damaging Brandon somehow.

There might not be much she could do if they found out Daniel McLean was Brandon's father, but for now, she'd try to learn as much as she could about him while maintaining her distance. Forewarned was forearmed.

Brandon and Daniel both disappeared into the room. Minutes later Daniel came back out.

"Brandon's hunting down the bucket of beanbags. This is it, though, right?" Daniel pointed to the big sheet of plywood, with a painted Santa with holes in the ball of his cap and three coat buttons. The paint was worn, and she could see the top half looked slightly off.

"That's it," she said with absolutely no enthusiasm. The toss was a mess.

Daniel nodded. "I could take it to my workshop and fix it faster than I could here. I have everything right there…the tools, the right setup."

"I was hoping you could just do something with glue."

Daniel waggled an end of the plywood that was held in place with only duct tape and a prayer.

"I see what you mean. But are you sure? It's not exactly spending time with Brandon, and I know that's why you signed on to help."

"No problem. I do want to spend time with Brandon, but…" He paused. "This won't take long to do at the shop. Do you mind if I ask Brandon to help me get it out to the truck?"

The question was considerate. Just another indication that Daniel McLean was a kind man. A man who would check with her before asking Brandon to do something. A man who was volunteering to do extra work that sometimes wouldn't allow him additional time with Brandon. They were all checks in the nice column. A perverse part of Michelle really wanted to find something about Daniel that wasn't so nice.

She'd just have to look harder. For now, she nodded. "That would be fine."

"Hey, Brandon," Daniel called. "Do you want to come get the doors for me? I'm taking Santa to my shop."

Brandon popped into the clearing. "Sure. Can I go there with you to your shop, too?"

"Well, I'm not going there now. I'm staying here to help your aunt. This project I can do faster at my place than here, is all."

"Oh."

Daniel lifted the Santa. "You got the door?"

Brandon held it open, and the two of them started down the hall.

Michelle followed them into the hallway and watched them go. She had what felt like a premonition.

Brandon would leave her.

The thought was almost a physical pain. She knew, in her head, that one day Brandon would grow up and be on his own, that he'd move away from her. But this was too soon.

Way too soon.

She forced herself to return to the storage room. She fell into the motion of checking things off her long list.

She found the huge box of holiday-wrapped coffee cans for the Chinese auction. She found the box of prizes that had started to trickle in, in response to the letter she'd sent out two weeks ago to local businesses. Mrs. Vioni, the office secretary, had the items sent down here. There were sweatshirts and other school items from the four local colleges—Mercyhurst, Gannon, Penn State Behrend and Edinboro. There was a beautiful wind chime from Nickel Plate Mills, and some great Erie prints donated by Burhenn's Pharmacy. She continued digging through the box, pleased by the community's response, and was busy cataloging the prizes when Brandon and Daniel came back in.

A rush of relief spread through her system.

Brandon was back.

She knew it was stupid. They'd only gone out to Daniel's truck, but still, there it was. Brandon was back beside her, where he belonged.

Unaware of her thoughts, Daniel simply smiled and asked, "Now what?"

Michelle handed him a sheet. "There's nothing at all organized about this room. These are the items I still need to find. Could you two look for them?"

Daniel scanned the list. "A Christmas tree? You use a fake tree? There's something so completely wrong about fake trees."

"For the school—" Michelle started.

Brandon interrupted. "But at home, we get a real one. Aunt Shell and I go to Burbules's Tree Farm and pick our own out. Then we come home, make hot chocolate, and I listen to her complain all afternoon as we try to get the tree to stand up straight in the stand, and she takes hours to put the balls on just right." Brandon had made teasing her about her decorating habits an annual sport, one he got better at each year.

"Hey, Bran, picking on the woman who has to make your dinner tonight probably isn't wise," she teasingly warned him. "I think I have some brussels sprouts in the freezer." She knew that was a dire threat in Brandon's eyes.

"Ugh," he groaned right on cue. "That's just mean, Aunt Shell. I'll eat most vegetables to keep you happy, but those little green things are just gross. You're being cruel."

"And picking on me because I want to make the tree straight and tidy isn't?"

"She likes everything straight and tidy," Brandon continued, obviously not intimidated in the least by her threats.

"Brussels sprouts," Michelle repeated. But he wasn't buying even her most menacing threats. He just laughed.

"Okay, Brandon, let's be systematic for your aunt's sake," Daniel said, a hint of teasing in his tone. He winked at Michelle to let her know the hint wasn't meant to be subtle. "Why don't you start in the west corner, and we'll go from there."

"Sure, anything to make things organized for Aunt Shell. Really, you should see her. Some year she's going to pull out a tape measurer so she can be sure those ornaments are evenly spaced," Brandon said with a chuckle as he took the list and headed into the back of the room.

Rather than follow him, Daniel came over to Michelle and asked in a low voice, "Instead of brussels sprouts, would you consider the two of you coming out to dinner with me? I didn't want to ask in front of Brandon, in case you couldn't."

Michelle realized what he meant was in case she *wouldn't*. He'd asked her privately so Brandon wouldn't be mad at her if she said no.

She tried not to let the small gesture touch her, but it did. Yet another check in the darned nice column.

Daniel waited for her reply and she could see in his eyes how much he wanted her to say yes, but that he doubted she would. It was a look Brandon gave her. And in that moment, she could see so much of her nephew in Daniel. That hurt, as well.

This wasn't about her, she reminded herself. It wasn't even

about Daniel. It was about Brandon, and he wanted to get to know this man. So, she replied, "Yes, that would be nice."

"Do you mind if I ask him where he'd like to go?"

"Go ahead. Though I'm pretty sure I can tell you his response."

Daniel disappeared into the storeroom. She heard him say, "Your aunt says we could all go out to dinner, if—" He didn't get any further because Brandon's whoop interrupted him.

"Do you have somewhere in particular you'd like to go?" Daniel continued.

"The Cornerstone," Brandon said immediately. "I love their burgers and it's not fancy or expensive."

"The Cornerstone it is."

An hour and a half later, they had found everything on Michelle's list. "I think that's it for today."

Daniel nodded at the cone-shaped foam object next to her. "What on earth is that?"

"It's a lollipop tree. You take a bag of suckers, color a few of the sticks at the bottom and push them in. The kids pay to draw out the suckers, and the ones that get the marked ones win a prize."

Daniel studied it a moment. "It's not very attractive in and of itself."

She shrugged. "No, but it serves its purpose." She gathered up her files and notes, and they all headed for the exit. "We'll meet you at the restaurant."

Brandon hung back. "Aunt Shell, can I ride with Daniel?"

It was only a few blocks. She had no reason to say no, as much as she'd like to. She thought of Samantha, and how her friend had worked so hard to get her ex back into their kids' lives. She'd done everything she could to facilitate a good relationship between them.

Samantha would say yes.

Michelle found herself nodding. "You don't mind?" she asked Daniel.

"No, of course I don't."

Brandon whooped again and headed for Daniel's truck.

"Thanks," Daniel said quietly to Michelle.

Michelle followed the truck. She could see Daniel nodding, presumably to something Brandon was saying.

She wondered what they were talking about. Was Brandon telling Daniel about his day? Filling him in on all the class happenings?

She was used to being his sounding board. Now, he had someone else who would listen.

She hated herself for being so petty. Daniel was willing to listen, and she concentrated on that fact rather than what she was missing out on.

The Cornerstone sat at the intersection of Thirty-Eighth Street and Pine Avenue. It was close to Mercyhurst College, and although the college kids frequented it, it still had a family air about it.

They got settled in the small dining area, and Brandon ordered his burger and fries. "And a house salad," he added as a concession to her vegetable-or-fruit-at-every-meal rule.

Michelle gave Brandon an approving smile as she placed her own order. Daniel ordered his meal, as well, and the waitress was back a few minutes later with their drinks.

The meal went smoothly. Brandon kept up a running commentary, forgetting the no-talking-with-food-in-your-mouth rule frequently. Finally, he wolfed down the remainder of his burger so he could talk without Michelle's auntly warning stares.

"And the chinchilla had babies, we think. She won't let them out of her box yet, but Mrs. Baker says she saw them. She put the dad in another cage 'cause he ate the last babies—"

"Bran," she complained.

"Sorry. No gross subjects at dinner," he told Daniel, then looked back to Michelle. "I can save them for after dinner, though, right, Aunt Shell?"

"You can save them indefinitely, as far as I'm concerned," she grumbled good-naturedly, which made him laugh.

They finished their meal and started gathering their coats. "I'll get to that beanbag toss right away," Daniel promised.

"There's no hurry," Michelle said. "Well, there is only two weeks, but it's not like you have to do it tonight."

"It will be done by the fair," he promised. "I'll see you two tomorrow around three again."

He said it as if it was a given.

Michelle felt uncomfortable again. Dinner had been casual and tension free. She'd enjoyed listening to Brandon's enthusiastic conversation. But suddenly, thinking about seeing Daniel tomorrow made her feel decidedly nervous.

She wasn't sure why her emotions were fluctuating back and forth, with no apparent reason, and she didn't know what to do about it.

They put their coats on and started for the door.

"You don't have to come every afternoon," she told him.

"I've already organized the next two weeks. It's one of the few perks of working for myself. I'm the boss, and so I set my own schedule."

He might be able to alter his hours, but she suspected he was having to make up for the time he spent with them, either by going to work early, or maybe he was planning to work after he went home. Either way, it had to be hard. But the look on his face was the same stubborn look Brandon often gave her.

Michelle just smiled. "Fine."

Their waitress gave them a friendly wave. "Thanks for coming. You have a beautiful family," she added.

Michelle didn't know what to say to that. She turned to look at Daniel, who simply turned around and said, "Thanks."

He walked Michelle and Brandon to the car. "About tomorrow. Rather than meeting at the school, would you two like to meet at my place? I have a few ideas for fixing up a few of the games and could use the help."

"Sure," Brandon said before Michelle had a chance to answer. "That would be cool, wouldn't it, Aunt Shell?" He looked at her with undisguised delight.

As much as she'd like to have said no, she couldn't. "That would be fine. I'll pick Brandon up after school and then we'll drive to your place."

"See you then," he said, and headed toward his truck.

"He's the coolest, isn't he, Aunt Shell? How long till we get the tests back?"

"A couple weeks, Bran," she told him for the umpteenth time. "Honey, you can't get your hopes up. Not until we know for sure."

"I know, I know. I need to be realistic." He echoed her own words.

Be realistic. It had sounded like good advice, but listening to Brandon parrot it, Michelle wasn't so sure. "Yes, let's both be realistic, but it's okay to hope."

She saw the happiness in his expression. "Yeah, I guess I can hope. 'Cause he's a nice guy. Just look how he took time off to help with the Christmas Fair, so he could spend time with me and I could get to know him."

"That was a nice thing."

"So, I'll be realistic, but I'll hope."

Despite her fears of losing Brandon and shaking up the life

they'd so painstakingly built, Michelle found herself hoping, for Brandon's sake, Daniel was his father after all.

"YOU HAVE A LOVELY FAMILY." The waitress's words echoed in Daniel's head all night. They'd left him feeling like a total fraud, and he hadn't known how to respond.

Michelle hadn't appeared to know what to say, either, so in the end he'd simply said, "Thanks."

Michelle and Brandon…they were a family.

He was the outsider. An interloper.

Even if he was Brandon's father, he wasn't sure where he'd fit in.

Chloe walked over and placed her head on his knee. He brushed the sawdust off her nose. "Occupational hazard when you come and help me out," he said aloud.

She wagged her tail encouragingly.

At about three in the morning he'd decided he wasn't going to get any more sleep, so he'd come out here to work. It was six now. He'd managed to get a lot done.

"I think they'll like them, don't you?"

Chloe wagged her tail again.

That was the nice thing about a dog, she pretty much always agreed with him.

He rubbed his hand through her winter-thick fur and tried to figure out what he wanted. Brandon was a great kid. Any man would be proud to be his father. But did Daniel want the hassle? He'd built a comfortable life, doing work he loved. He had Chloe for companionship.

Life was simple. He didn't answer to anyone, and no one counted on him. He never had to fear letting someone down.

That's how he liked it. He should be praying with every fiber of his being that Brandon wasn't his son.

And yet…

You have a lovely family.

When the waitress had said the words, he'd wished he could claim Brandon and Michelle as his family. For just that briefest moment, he'd wanted it desperately. Even though he knew his family track record was less than stellar.

Knowing what he should want, and not wanting what he shouldn't want—that wasn't always easy.

The head might understand what was best, but the heart didn't always listen.

Chapter Six

It would be easier for Michelle if she didn't like Daniel McLean. She'd be able to tell herself that she was going along with his seeing Brandon just in case he was Brandon's father.

But since she did like him, it was hard to tell how much of her decision to be here today was because it was best for Brandon, and how much was because being in Daniel's company was easy.

Very easy.

Too easy.

"Aunt Shell?" Brandon's tone said whatever he was going to ask next was important to him.

"Yes, Bran?"

"What should I call him?"

She didn't need to ask him who they were talking about. "What do you want to call him?"

She glanced at him in the passenger seat. His hair, as usual, was a tousled mess. And he wore a perplexed expression, as if wrangling with a question of the utmost import. "Well, Mr. McLean doesn't sound really right."

"Too formal," she agreed.

She made the soft left from Wattsburg Road onto Old Wattsburg Road.

"I tried Daniel, but that's what everyone else calls him," Brandon said.

"And you want something different?" Michelle asked.

He nodded. "I think, if he doesn't mind, I'd like to call him Dan."

"Why don't you ask him to be sure."

She quickly looked at him and he nodded. "Okay, I will."

She made the left onto Daniel's road, and about a half mile later, turned into Daniel's driveway.

"Come on, Aunt Shell," Brandon cried as he bolted from the car the moment she put it into Park.

Chloe ran out from behind the house to greet him. Brandon was immediately down on the ground, rolling around with her in the snow. Michelle sat in the car watching the two of them before she got out. The sight made her smile.

They were both covered in snow and, when Brandon sat up, Chloe backed off him and shook. Snow flew everywhere.

Her smile evaporated as Daniel came out of the barn. He walked over to Brandon, who immediately forgot about the dog and got up, watching this man he hoped was his father.

Michelle got out of the car.

"Hey," Brandon said by way of a greeting to Daniel.

"Hey, Brandon." Daniel looked at Michelle as she approached them. "Michelle, hi—"

Brandon interrupted. "I know you said I could call you Daniel, but I talked to Aunt Shell and she said if it was okay with you, I could call you Dan."

"That's what they called my grandfather. I was named after him. Everyone called me Daniel to differentiate between us. I always thought it was better than being called Little Dan. I'd be proud to have you call me by his name."

"I mean, if you are my dad, Dan is awfully close to Dad, so it won't be a hard change."

He hadn't mentioned that part of it to Michelle, but she could tell he'd thought long and hard about it.

Daniel agreed. "You're right, Dan is awfully close to Dad."

"So, if you are my dad, you won't mind me calling you Dad?"

Daniel knelt so that he was eye level with Brandon. "Son, any man would be lucky to have you calling him Dad." Daniel stopped, seemingly unsure what to say next.

Michelle took pity and stepped in. "Well, Daniel, why don't you show us what progress you've made."

"That sounds like a good idea." He led them to the barn. "Come on in."

As she entered the barn, Michelle saw two giant wooden panels with holes in them leaning against a workbench.

"I hope you don't mind. Your old beanbag toss was beat. I thought it might be time for an upgrade. I have the wood all sanded, and thought you two might help me paint one with a Santa. I already sketched it. And I thought, just to switch things up, we'd do a snowman, as well. I made the holes a lot smaller on him, so it's more challenging for older kids. When we've got them painted, I'll put a few coats of a sealant on them. They should last the school for years."

"Daniel, you spent so much time. I thought maybe you could just slap some staples or some more glue on the other one, and fix it. I didn't imagine you taking time to do not just one, but two new ones."

"Slapping some staples and glue onto a project to hold it together isn't how I do things. Imagine what it would do to my reputation," he teased.

"Well, thank you. We can certainly help with the painting."

Before they got started, she took another look around

Daniel's shop. She wasn't a woodworker, but if she was, it would be paradise.

There had to be a dozen big machines. Saws she could recognize, but some were out of her league. Huge workbenches. Vises. And a giant Peg-Board with tools of every shape and description hung neatly.

"This is amazing," she said. "It's even more amazing than the first time we saw it the other day."

Brandon called. "Hey, *Dan,* I can start painting?"

Michelle could tell he was trying out the name on Dan, and from his happy expression, she gathered he was pleased with it.

"Sure," Daniel said easily. "Let's get you set up."

Michelle watched as Daniel got an old shirt and put it over Brandon's clothes. Then he laid the snowman beanbag toss on the ground, opened a can of paint and got him started.

Brandon dipped the paintbrush into the can, then stopped, the paintbrush dripping over the can. "What if I do it wrong?"

"Well, if you like how you paint it, then it's not wrong."

"But what if I don't? What if I make a huge mistake?"

Michelle started to answer, but decided to hold her tongue and let Daniel take the question.

"Then we'll fix it," he said with no hesitation. "My grandpa used to say, 'Mistakes are like rocks. If you try to drop them, you're bound to hit your own foot and it'll hurt. But if you study them carefully and put them in the creek, you'll eventually have enough to get to the other side.'"

Brandon looked confused. "What does that mean?"

"Well, my grandpa had a lot of sayings, and none of them were really clear, but I always thought this one meant, if you try to get rid of your mistakes by ignoring them, they're bound to end up hurting you. However, if you take them out, and study them carefully, trying to figure out where you went wrong, then you can use them as a stepping stone to new things."

"So, if I make a mistake painting?" Brandon persisted.

"If you do, then we'll correct it and the next time you start painting, you'll do it just a bit better. You can't learn anything without making a few mistakes. That's what my grandma used to say. She was more to the point than my grandfather."

"They sound nice." There was a wistfulness in Brandon's voice that tore at Michelle. "I have a grandma, but she doesn't live here, and doesn't visit much. She just sends me a present on my birthday and Christmas."

"I'm sorry," Daniel said.

Brandon shrugged. "Aunt Shell says she loves me in her own way. That you can't make someone love you the way you want, that you just have to take what they can give and accept it."

"Your aunt is a very smart lady."

"Yeah, I think so, too," Brandon assured him. Then more loudly, he said, "But don't tell her I said that, 'cause she'll remind me of that next time I want to do something and she has to say no."

"I won't tell," Daniel promised, looking back at Michelle and winking. "But I suspect your aunt already knows how smart she is."

"Sure, she's real good with math. I mean, most of the kids' moms and dads can't help them with math homework, but Aunt Shell always can. And she can explain it better than the teacher. So, I go home, ask her, then show my friends the next day before class."

Brandon started painting in the snowman's bottom snowball.

Daniel turned around and looked at Michelle. "I have something else to show you."

"My, you were busy last night."

"I didn't sleep well, so I worked," he admitted as they walked across the workshop.

"I didn't sleep well, either," she told him.

He went over to a the workbench, and reached underneath it and pulled out a wooden Christmas tree. It was composed of graduated stars, stacked one on top of the other on a thick wooden dowel, the biggest at the bottom and gradually getting smaller toward the top. The ends of the stars had holes drilled in them. "Your foam tree was a little beat-up, too. I've got this green stain, and then with a few coats of polyurethane, you'll have a sucker tree—"

"That will last for years," she finished for him. She ran a hand over the bottom star. The wood was sanded to a silky smoothness. "You like making things to last."

"It's what I've built my business on. The antique pieces that I restore… Hopefully my repairs will help them remain for future generations."

Michelle had a sudden burst of insight. "You're a dreamer." She hadn't meant to say it out loud, and hadn't even realized she'd done so until she saw Daniel's expression.

"Pardon?"

Now that she'd said it, she had to explain. "You don't live just in the here and now, you live in the past and the future. A dreamer."

She felt embarrassed by the explanation.

"And what are you?" he asked.

"I'm a realist. I live in the here and now. I deal with the concrete. That's why I like numbers. They're solid. They're always the same. One and one always equals two. I like that certainty."

"When I was in college, I thought I was a realist, as well. I followed my grandfather's advice and was a business major.

Business was something you could count on. That's what he wanted for me. Stability. Then I met your sister and she taught me to dream."

THE MINUTE he mentioned Tara, Daniel knew he'd made a mistake. He could almost see Michelle physically shut him out. It was as if a wall had gone up.

"Yes," she said. "Tara was a dreamer. It didn't matter who she hurt getting what she dreamed of. My whole life has been spent picking up the pieces of Tara's broken dreams."

"Michelle, I'm—" He started to apologize, but she cut him off.

"If you find me that stain, I'll get to work on this. You can help Brandon paint."

He'd been dismissed.

He wanted to talk to her about Tara, but clearly Michelle wasn't in the mood, so he let it go.

"The stain's right here." He pointed to the small container on a nearby workbench. "I left out gloves, a sponge brush and a rag. Just brush the stain on, wait a minute and wipe it off with the rag."

She nodded and picked up the gloves. "I can handle it. Go spend time with Brandon. That's why we're here, right?"

"Yes, I guess it is." And it was. He was spending time with Michelle and Brandon in order to get to know the boy who might be his son. But there was something about Michelle that made him want to know her better. He wanted to talk about Tara, wanted Michelle to open up to him again, and he wasn't sure why.

Having an amicable relationship with Brandon's aunt was going to be important if Brandon was his son, but that wasn't the reason he wanted to spend more time with her.

He liked her.

It was that simple.

But she was already busy sponging on the stain, ignoring him. So he left her to it and joined Brandon, who was meticulously painting in his outline. "This is going to be so cool, Dan. Do you think, sometime, you'd let me help with the tools, not just the painting?"

"Sure, if you want to learn to use some of the tools, I can show you. We'd have to check with your aunt, but as long as you follow the safety rules, you'd be fine. And the first safety rule in my shop is don't touch any of the power tools without my express permission. Some of them can be dangerous. Actually, I guess all of them can be dangerous, if you don't know what you're doing. I wasn't much older than you when I started working in the wood shop."

"You learned when you were my age?" Brandon asked.

"My grandfather worked for the city streets department, plowing the roads in the winter, filling potholes and that kind of thing. But when he got home, he'd head to the garage and make things. He was a talented carpenter. He didn't do furniture and renovation work, but he did a lot of carving. He especially liked Santas. I've got a whole cabinet full of them, and some of the other things he made, in the house."

"Can you show me?"

"Sure. When we're done here, if you like and your aunt says it's okay." He tried to be careful to not step on Michelle's toes. She was in charge of Brandon. He wasn't sure how that would change if he found out he was Brandon's father. Would she consider sharing custody with him? Would she let him take an active role in Brandon's life? And what if she wouldn't? Would he be willing to fight for his rights?

He glanced at her systematically staining the tree. She'd been accommodating so far, but right now he was temporary. What if he was permanent?

"Well, if you are my dad," Brandon said, echoing his own thoughts, "that would make your grandpa my great-grandfather and I'd like to know about him." The boy paused. "Do you think he would have liked me?"

"I'm sure he would have. He was a nice man. And talented at what he did."

"Was he happy you were going to be a carpenter?"

Daniel had just told Michelle this story, and turned to see if she was listening. But she was intent on staining and far enough away that he wasn't even sure if she could hear, so he told it again. "My grandfather wanted me to be a businessman. He thought it would make a more secure job. It was your mom who told me I shouldn't worry about what was safe. I should follow my dream instead."

"She did that?"

"She did."

Brandon nodded and looked as if he was digesting the new fact about his mother.

Daniel finally said, "Tell me, what sort of things do you like to do…when you're not painting snowmen and Santas? I have a whole list of things I'd like to know. Do you play sports? Do you like to read?"

"I just finished *Lord of the Rings*. I liked the movies, and Aunt Shell said the books were even better, and they were. At least, once I got used to the way Tolkien wrote. It was…"

"More formal," Daniel supplied. "I remember that from when I read them. Your aunt was right, the movies were great, but the books were better. I'm glad you like books. I can't remember when I wasn't reading something."

"You can thank Aunt Shell for that. When I was little, right after I came to live with her, she let me stay up an extra half hour if I read."

"And so you read?"

Brandon laughed. "Yeah, or she'd read to me. She liked fairy tales, even though I kept telling her they were for girls. They all started with *once upon* and ended with *happily ever after.* That's not a boy thing." He shot a look at Michelle.

"After a while," Brandon continued, "I'd find a book that I couldn't wait to read the rest of, so I'd read during the day, and now, I just read whenever I get a chance."

"Well, we've already covered that your aunt's a smart lady."

"She is. She worries a lot, though." Brandon's eyebrows creased with concern as he said the words.

"About what?"

"When I first came, she worried 'cause she was so young. And she worried about me, that all Mom's moving around had made me insecure, and that Mom's dying was going to hurt me for a long time, so she had me go talk to a psychiatrist. She went, too. Said it was family therapy, even though there were only two of us."

"Did it make you mad?"

"Nah. The doctor was nice, and she helped me and Aunt Shell figure out how to be a family. Poor Aunt Shell. She'd just got out of school and started her accounting job at A&D Financial, then Mom shows up with me, and she'd never even told Aunt Shell about me. I figure that had to be hard, watching her sister die, then having to deal with a kid she didn't even know about."

Daniel was touched by Brandon's empathy. "I'm sure it was hard on her, but it must have been hard on you, too."

"I loved Mom, really, but…" He paused.

"You can tell me," Daniel assured him. "No matter what that test shows, I hope we'll always be friends."

"Well, Mom moved around a lot. I never went to the same school for too long. I never got to make many friends. I don't have any of my old toys or anything, because when we moved, I normally just got my suitcase. When I came to live with Aunt Shell…well, everything is always the same. You always put your shoes on the mat in the hallway. There's a hook there I always hang my coat on. My bedroom's always my bedroom, and Aunt Shell and I always clean and she does the laundry on Saturday mornings. Things are just always the same."

"And that's good?" he asked.

"It's nice to know you'll be sleeping in your bed, in your room."

Daniel realized that Brandon was talking about stability. He had that with Michelle. She'd given him a sense of belonging somewhere.

He got that. As much as he'd missed his mother, he'd found that same sense of belonging with his grandparents.

"Sometimes Aunt Shell still worries too much. When she does a job, like this Christmas Fair. She'll worry until she has everything organized, and it will be good. But she worries so much about me, sometimes I feel like…" He shrugged. "I love her, and I owe her a lot. But there are things I want to do, and she's too worried to let me. I play soccer, and I want to play hockey, but—"

"She's worried?"

"Yeah. There are tryouts for a developmental league next week, and I really want to try, even though I'd be kinda old, but Aunt Shell will say no. Maybe you could talk to her?"

Oh, this was tricky ground here. Daniel had been careful, so very careful, not to step on Michelle's toes. He wanted her to trust him enough to let him into the life she'd built with Brandon. He sensed she wouldn't want her rules and concerns for Brandon questioned. "I don't know, Bran."

"But if you're my dad, you'd have a say."

"We won't know that for a while yet, and your aunt Shell has raised you all these years. She's got a lot more experience than I do." That was an understatement. Daniel had grown up an only child, and hadn't spent any time with kids since he was a child himself.

"But even if you knew you were my dad, you wouldn't want to make her let me play hockey." It was a statement more than a question.

He sounded so defeated. Daniel knew how he felt. He'd learned woodworking at his grandfather's knee and, rather than go to college, he'd wanted to go into contracting, something where he'd get to use his hands. His grandfather had insisted he attend college, had pushed him into business. At the time he'd resented it. He'd chaffed under his grandfather's heavy hand. But now?

That business degree had proved invaluable to him.

"I can't and won't tell your aunt what to do, but if the opportunity arises, and she doesn't mind my input, I'll try and speak to her."

"Great." Brandon grinned. "Thanks, Dan."

"Hey, how are things going over here?" Michelle was standing next to them, examining the beanbag toss.

Daniel looked down and saw that they'd finished. "The snowman's done, which leaves us Santa."

"The Christmas tree's done, as well."

"We're almost finished for the night." Daniel felt a spurt of regret. He didn't want them to go. "Listen, I don't know what you two planned, but I put a beef stew in the Crock-Pot, and thought you might like to stay for dinner. I mean, you worked all day, then came here and I thought you might like the break."

He thought Michelle was going to thank him but say no. He

could see it in her expression. Then Brandon said, "Please, Aunt Shell?"

Michelle's expression softened. "Sure. If you're certain it won't be an imposition."

"Not at all."

The Santa didn't take long to paint with all three of them working on it. Daniel loved listening to Brandon and Michelle tease each other.

"Oh, no, Aunt Shell. Is that a spot of paint on your shirt?"

Michelle checked, which set Brandon laughing. "Come on, Aunt Shell. You never get spots of anything, but you always fall for it when I say you do."

A few minutes later, Michelle had given an Oscar-winning girly shriek, and pointed just behind Brandon, who'd jumped up and spun around. "Revenge is sweet," she'd said in a pretty good villain's voice, then cackled.

"You'd better watch out for her, Dan, she always gets her revenge."

"I can see that."

They'd finished and headed inside. The moment they'd entered the kitchen, before anyone had even taken off a coat, Chloe dropped her ball at Brandon's feet. "She's hoping you'll play with her."

"I'm not allowed to throw balls in the house."

"And that's a very good rule, but maybe you could take her out back and throw it for a bit while I make the biscuits?"

"Is that okay, Aunt Shell?" Brandon asked.

She smiled. "Go on."

MICHELLE FELT awkward being alone with Daniel. He didn't seem to mind in the least as he busied himself, turning on the oven then taking a tube out of the refrigerator.

"It was kind of you to invite us," she said when the silence had grown too weighty. "Uh, I don't want you to think you need to feed us every day."

"Michelle, it was kind of you to say yes. I can understand your hesitancy. Really, I can. But I want to spend time with Brandon. I want to get to know him."

"In case he's your son," she clarified.

Daniel nodded as he thwacked the tube of biscuits against the edge of the counter. It gave a loud pop as it split. "But there's more to it than that. He's an amazing kid. The fact that he found me, that he came out and met me—"

"On his own. A dangerous and stupid thing," she pointed out.

"But he stayed on the porch and wouldn't even take a ride from me. He's smart. He's responsible. He's Tara's son." He paused as he placed the round doughy discs on the cookie sheet. "I still can't believe she's gone."

Michelle felt for him. "Neither can I. She was the most…"

She searched for a word to describe her sister. "Alive. She was the most alive person I've ever met. She was terminally happy and optimistically sure that something wonderful was around the next corner. People were drawn to her, like moths to flame. The only problem, like a flame, she didn't ever consider that the people who were close to her got burned. Even her son."

"He seems okay." Dan looked up from the biscuits, his concern evident in his expression.

"He does, and he is okay. There are moments, though, things he's said that worry me. I took him to a therapist when he first came to live with me."

"He told me. He said that you both went."

"I didn't know how to parent and wanted all the help I could get. I was young."

"You're not actually old now." He smiled.

"No, I'm not actually old now. But I'm getting there—every day a little closer. This parenting stuff can age you quick." She was kidding, but there was truth to her words. She felt so much older than twenty-nine.

Friends from college were still out partying on weekends. They were starting to find partners, marry, even have babies. She was parenting a teenager.

"I imagine that parenting can age you. I'm already worried about him. Worried about how he's really handling everything, worrying there's more I could do to make it easier." Dan looked embarrassed by his admission, and quickly turned to put the tray into the oven. When he faced Michelle again, he simply said, "He's a great kid, though."

"He is," she agreed.

Daniel went and looked out the window, then motioned Michelle to join him. Brandon had discarded the ball and was throwing snowballs for Chloe, who couldn't figure out where the "balls" were disappearing to as they fell into and blended with the snow on the ground. It was obvious that Brandon found the game amusing, as he tossed snowball after snowball.

Chloe finally had enough and charged at Brandon, sending him flying backward into the snow, snowflakes flying. She promptly licked the remnants off his face.

"I see a lot of me in him," Daniel said softly.

"He's a great kid, so he's like you?" she teased.

He laughed. "Well, there's that. But seriously, what I mean is, I had parents who cared more for their own wants and desires than what was best for me. I was lucky that I landed here with Grams and Pops. And Brandon was equally lucky that he landed with you. Despite a rough start, we had people who loved us. That makes all the difference. We share that. You're good for him."

The buzzer rang. "The biscuits are done. You want to go call him in?"

"Sure." She opened the door and Chloe spotted her and charged into the kitchen with the ball in her mouth, Brandon close at her heels.

"She's fast, Dan." He panted as hard as the dog.

"She is. She loves having someone to run with. Thanks. You saved me from throwing the ball after dinner."

"Anytime you want me to, I can help out with Chloe." Brandon leaned down and started to take off his boots. While he was precariously perched on one foot, Chloe bumped him, sent him sprawling, then started licking him again.

"Looks like Chloe would enjoy you helping with her." Dan opened up the cupboard and took out three deep bowls and three plates. "I'm not very formal. I thought we could eat in here, if that's okay."

"That's fine," Michelle assured him.

Daniel was efficient, she noticed. He dished up the bowls, poured Brandon a glass of milk and opened a bottle of wine. "It's from Noble Winery, just over the border in New York."

Michelle took a sip of the deep red liquid. "I confess I don't know much about wine, but this is good."

"I don't, either. Although, I think I'm developing a bit of a palate because I'm enjoying semidries more than sweet these days. My friend Jimmy is big-time into wine. He gave me a list of wineries in the area, and whenever I'm out that way, I try to stop. I've got quite a nice local collection. I'm always thrilled when someone's over to share a bottle, since I'm not enough of a wine drinker to finish one off on my own."

"One glass is my limit," Michelle said.

They ate in silence for a few minutes, then Daniel said, "So, Brandon, tell me about school. I'd love to hear more about your classmates, your teachers and your classes."

Brandon launched into a who's who of his class and teachers, then segued off into a who-did-what-where-and-when description of his day. He told Daniel about his test results, and a surprise quiz he aced.

Michelle listened to the two of them back-and-forthing. Daniel, so eager to know Brandon, and Brandon positively glowing under Daniel's attention.

She hadn't considered how much her nephew had needed a man's presence in his life. It had been easy to pretend the two of them were self-sufficient, that they didn't need anyone else. But becoming friends with Samantha and Carly these past few months had shown her that acquaintances and fellow employees weren't enough. Even Heidi, whom she'd considered a friend, was more a friendly acquaintance. She was someone Michelle might have coffee with, but if Michelle was stranded at three in the morning and needed a ride, she'd hesitate to call Heidi and wake her.

She wouldn't hesitate calling Samantha or Carly. And she knew that either of them would drop everything to come get her.

Yes, she needed friends. She needed Carly and Samantha. And it was obvious that Brandon needed more than she could give him. He needed a man in his life. Not just any man. He wanted Daniel McLean.

If Daniel wasn't Brandon's father, Bran was going to be crushed. And it was too late to pull him back. Too late to save him from that potential pain.

They finished the meal, and Michelle insisted she and Brandon help do the dishes. "We have a rule at our house, everyone helps."

"And by everyone, she means me," Brandon mock-groused.

Daniel just thwacked Brandon with a towel. "Come on, then."

When they'd finished, Michelle was ready to hustle Brandon out the door, but before she could get her coat, he said, "Before we go, Dan, could you show me those Santas your grandpa carved?" He turned to Michelle. "Dan learned about wood from his grandpa. His grandpa carved all kinds of Santas, and he made other stuff, too, right, Dan?"

"Yes." He glanced at Michelle. "It will only take a few minutes."

"Okay."

She followed Brandon and Daniel. They went to what had to be Daniel's study. There was a built-in cabinet along one wall. Daniel flipped a switch at one side, and illuminated the glass shelves that were lined with Santas. She'd never seen anything like it. There was a police officer Santa, a woodworking Santa. Tall ones, fat ones…a skiing one, a golfing one. "He loved doing this kind of thing. He was—"

"An artist," Michelle assured him.

Daniel looked pleased at her comment. "Yes, he was. He'd have never thought of himself as one, but he was." He walked to the center of the cabinet and took out two Santas. "These are my favorites. Grandpa also had a huge passion for the Civil War, so he combined those two things and got these."

"A North and South Santa." He handed one to Brandon.

"Yes. A Union soldier Santa, and a Confederate soldier Santa."

"They're so cool, Dan," Brandon said, turning the carving over in his hand, admiring it.

"They are. I sometimes forget how cool they are. I guess I get complacent. Thanks for reminding me, Brandon."

"You said you had other things your grandpa made?"

Michelle could tell how much Brandon didn't want the night to end. He'd keep asking questions and stalling for as long as she allowed. "Brandon, I really think we've taken up enough of Daniel's time today. And I know you've got homework."

"Yeah."

"Maybe I could show them to you next time you're here? It will give you something to look forward to," promised Daniel, coming to her aid.

"That would be good. The next time," Brandon repeated, looking at Michelle.

She could see that he wanted her to reassure him there would be a next time, so she said, "Daniel's right, it will be something to look forward to the next time."

Brandon was suddenly all smiles as they went back to the kitchen and gathered their boots and coats.

"Aunt Shell, could we go skating this weekend with Dan? I want to show him my moves."

Everything in Michelle wanted to say no. No, you're getting too close, too fast to this practical stranger. But she could see the longing in Brandon's eyes and there was nothing in her that was able to say no to that. "Daniel, we'd understand if you were busy," she tried, praying he'd say they'd taken up too much of his time already, that he was going to spend his weekend catching up on work.

Instead, he smiled. "No, I'm not busy at all. If you're sure you don't mind, I can make time."

"Then Saturday morning?"

"That sounds great. And in the meantime, I'll be at Erie Elementary right around three tomorrow."

It was a promise. And Michelle realized she wasn't dreading Daniel coming tomorrow. Maybe she should be. Maybe she should still be worried, knowing that Brandon was growing too attached. Yet she couldn't seem to find any worries or concern as she smiled and said, "We'll see you then."

Chapter Seven

Michelle spotted Samantha and Carly as she set up a table on the stage. "What are you two doing here?"

Her words came out sharper than she'd intended. She'd been curt all day, and she blamed it on her sleepless night. Daniel McLean haunted her dreams, so she'd tried to avoid falling asleep.

After last night's painting and dinner, she should have been having nightmares, worrying about Daniel's growing relationship with her nephew.

Instead, she'd had a lurid dream that featured her and Daniel…and had nothing at all to do with her nephew.

"Sorry guys. Not enough sleep last night." Her apology didn't seem enough. "It's a nice surprise seeing you here. But really, I know you both have other things to do."

"Harry said you were working on the crafts today, and I like crafts." Samantha flushed slightly as she mentioned Harry's name. That's all it took—just saying his name—for her to get all romantic.

Most of the time, Michelle felt happy whenever she thought about Samantha falling so suddenly for Harry, but today, she didn't want to think about falling, or going all romantic over a guy. She was in too crabby a mood for even someone else's love to brighten it.

Carly didn't bother to offer up an excuse as to why she was here. She simply said, "You look like hell."

"Carly," Samantha admonished their dark-haired spitfire of a friend, then turned to Michelle and admitted, "Uh, you do look a *little* tired."

"I am. Like I said, rough night." They didn't seem convinced, so she added, "That's all."

"Did this guy do something?" Carly had a look that said if "this guy" had, he'd regret it.

Given Carly's recent brush with the law, Michelle would have lied if necessary, but it wasn't. Her weird dreams weren't Daniel's fault. Daniel had been nothing but consistently kind and helpful.

"No. He's actually been great," Michelle admitted.

"I guess we'll see how great he is," Carly assured her. "We're here to help, but it will also give me a chance to check him out."

"Carly, honestly," Samantha said in a very impressive motherly voice.

"Like she wouldn't have figured out why we're here," Carly grumbled. "It's not like Michelle couldn't handle the crafts on her own. I've never seen anyone so…well, capable. But capable doesn't mean you don't need friends scoping out the new guy."

"Speak for yourself," said Samantha, still in a scolding voice. "I don't need to check him out, remember? I met him on Monday and told you he seemed very nice."

Carly snorted. "I'd prefer making my own assessment, thank you. So, where do I start, Michelle?"

"By putting your coats on and leaving?" Michelle assured herself that she was teasing—well, mostly teasing.

Samantha gave her a look of sympathy. "There was no talking her out of this."

"No, there wasn't, Samantha, and no I'm not leaving, Michelle."

"Harry promised to entertain the kids, and we're here to do whatever's needed."

"I brought a couple crafts." Carly held out a huge plastic bag. "I know we're always running short of gifts that the kids can buy for their families."

"Thank goodness. I don't have a crafty bone in my body," Michelle assured her. She knew there were some leftover beads and fishing line for necklaces from last year that she'd planned to work on today, but even that might have stretched her to her crafty limits.

"Well, though most people don't believe it, I do," Carly said. "I have a whole body of crafty bones. For instance…" She opened the bag and pulled out a huge bag of what appeared to be orange juice lids. "These will be very cute punched-tin ornaments when you're done. All you need is a basic pattern, a nail and a hammer. And this…" She held a bag of pipe cleaners, and a couple spools of glittery thread. "These will be ornaments. I thought we'd do a bunch for the younger kids, and the older ones can do the craft on their own. And I printed a poem that goes with them."

She took out a stack of red and green papers and read the top one.

"I'm a little spider.
No matter where I roam,
I'm lucky, for you see
I'm never far from home.
So put me in your Christmas tree,
I'll make a pretty guest.
My web will shine and sparkle there
Along with all the rest."

She pulled another stack of papers from her bag. "And here's a great legend, *The Christmas Spider*. I stapled the pages together into a booklet form. The kids will each get one when they buy the spider ornament, and they can color the pictures in it and give it along with the ornaments."

"You are a crafty goddess," Samantha said in awe and gave a mock bow.

"I like making things." Carly shrugged. "I don't know what it is about me that makes people think I'm not very domestic. I love to cook, and crochet."

"I don't know. Maybe it's the arson charge?" Samantha teased.

"Hey, accidental arson, if you please?" Carly insisted with a grin. "And before you ask, yes, everything's still fine with that. Henry Rizzo called and my hearing's the same day as the Christmas Fair."

"I wanted to be there for you—" Michelle was desperately trying to decide how she could manage the Christmas Fair from a distance, even as Samantha said, "I'll be there."

Carly shook her head. "I appreciate that, both of you. But Michelle, you're running the fair, and Samantha, we're a committee. Someone needs to be here helping Michelle. Henry assures me this is a formality. The judge just has to rubber-stamp the plea deal. I've already paid restitution, and if I don't commit any more accidental arsons, they'll eventually erase the conviction. Since I never plan to marry again, there's no worries about being cheated on and needing to burn another couch." She was trying to make a joke of the incident, but Michelle knew how badly Carly had been hurt by her ex and her heart ached for her friend.

"It's first thing Christmas Fair morning," Carly continued. "So, I'll get that out of the way, then be here in time to help with lunch."

Every year, volunteers working the Christmas Fair were treated to a potluck lunch. In addition, Michelle had called Urbaniak's a couple weeks ago, and they were very generously donating a meat-and-cheese platter. The neighborhood meat market had always been willing to help out Erie Elementary. As for the potluck part, the mothers would each bring a dish. She'd already sent a sheet around.

"So, what do you want to start on?" Carly apparently wanted to change the subject. "Spiders or punch-tin ornaments?"

Michelle didn't press her, but simply said, "Why don't we do the spiders? I think the ornaments are pretty straightforward. Punching holes. Even I can do that. The spiderweb thing sounds more complex."

Carly ran them through the very basic design. Black pipe cleaners made the spokes, and the glittery thread was the webbing itself. The spider was a black foam half-ball with little googly eyes glued on, and pipe cleaner legs.

After a couple attempts, Michelle and Samantha got the hang of it, though their spiders for some reason didn't look as good as Carly's. But Carly seemed satisfied, and must have decided they'd progressed enough to weave webs and talk. "So, tell us about Daniel."

Michelle had known it was coming, and had been mentally preparing her response. "He's sweet. He's a gifted artist. He'd probably say craftsman, if asked, but I've seen his work—he's an artist. He's kind. He's got a good sense of humor, and he makes a mean stew. To be honest, if circumstances were different, I might like him a lot."

Samantha stopped winding her spool of thread. "Why can't you like him a lot now?"

"This whole thing with Brandon is complicated enough. I

wouldn't consider becoming attracted to Daniel and muddying the waters even more."

"Oh, you meant, *like,*" Carly said. "*Like,* as in ooh, that man's so hot, sort of like."

"I didn't say that, and as I said, I don't plan to *like* him. I have to keep my distance."

"Have to? Or is it just safer to?" Samantha pushed. "You can't control who you're attracted to."

"Sure I can." Michelle knew her friend didn't want to hear it, but she could.

Samantha and Carly laughed.

"I can," Michelle insisted.

"I didn't want to fall for Harry, and yet…" Samantha shrugged. "Love happens."

"How did we get onto the subject of love?" Michelle asked. "We were talking about attraction, and how I'm not going to allow myself to be attracted to Daniel McLean, no matter how wonderful he seems. I can guarantee you that love wasn't even in the realm of consideration." She wound the glittery thread around the pipe cleaner with far more force than was required.

"I'm with Michelle on this one, Samantha, at least about the love part," Carly said. "Even though you're all head over heels and topsy-turvy in love, that doesn't mean the rest of us are going to fall. I tried my hand at love, and it so did not work. I'm not planning to go that route again. Although, unlike our Michelle, a little attraction and a whole lot of lust are definitely on my list of possibilities."

The sound of a throat clearing had all three PTA parents turning around and catching sight of Harry and Daniel. "Sorry to interrupt, but we're here to help."

"Pardon?"

"Daniel and I stored the new beanbag tosses and lollipop tree and we thought we'd lend a hand with the crafting."

Samantha looked at Harry with skepticism in her eyes. "Really?"

"Are you doubting my crafting abilities, woman?"

"Hey, don't feel bad, Harry," Carly said. "They doubted mine. Seems a little bit of arson—"

"Accidental arson," Michelle reminded her. "It wouldn't do to forget that important part when you're up in front of the judge."

"Right. It seems a little bit of *accidental* arsonage leaves your friends doubting your ability to craft."

"Should I even ask?" Daniel stage-whispered to Michelle as he sat down next to her.

He was a little too close for comfort, especially considering the recent conversation. Michelle couldn't think of any way to put distance between them without being obvious, so she sat still.

"Of course you should ask," Carly told him. "Long story short, I caught my rat-bastard husband—who's now my ex, by the way—on a couch I'd spent months shopping for with his very clichéd secretary. I won that couch in the divorce settlement. And I decided to purge all my anger and bitterness, and start the new year fresh by burning it. The couch, I mean. So, as I burned the couch, hoping to put the past behind me, my shed accidentally caught fire."

"Oh, accidental arson," Daniel said.

Carly nodded. "And my shed set my neighbor's shed on fire."

"Ouch," Daniel said sympathetically.

"Well, my neighbor was very nice about it. I paid for a new one and replaced all his tools and stuff, but it seems the law isn't quite as forgiving. Although, the ADA gave me a deal, and my appearance in court the morning of the Christmas Fair is a requirement."

"I have one more question, if you don't mind?" Daniel asked.

Michelle caught the smallest hint of a smile as he asked. Carly nodded.

"Was it worth it? Do you feel as if your past is behind you at this point?"

"You know, I do. Or at least I will as soon as I have my day in front of the judge in a week and a half."

"A week and a half until the fair. We'd better get going on these crafts," Michelle said, hoping to take the focus off Carly. Despite her cavalier attitude, she had to be worried about the hearing.

Carly gave Harry and Daniel instructions, and they all went on to work on their pipe cleaner spiders and webs, talking and laughing as they did.

The kids ran amok in the gym. Shooting hoops, playing tag. Even doing homework.

About five, they began clearing up the mess, a healthy pile of spiders sitting on webs to show for their afternoon's work.

As Daniel and Harry carried the folding table and chairs to the back of the stage, Michelle turned to her friends. "Thanks for coming in and helping."

"The Social Planning Committee is just that…a committee. We're here to help. No one expects you to do it all." Samantha dropped her voice. "You're right, he's nice."

"Very nice," Carly echoed softly.

The guys came back. "We'll go round up the kids," Harry said. "Come on, Daniel. You start on the left, I'll start on the right."

Daniel followed Harry down onto the gym floor and soon the men were grabbing basketballs and storing them as they prodded kids into collecting coats, boots and book bags.

"Yes, he is nice," Michelle agreed with a sigh.

"Do you need us tomorrow?" Carly asked.

"No. I'm going to do the actual shopping tomorrow, I think."

"As much as no one can believe I'm crafty," Carly said, "I need to point out I don't shop. Unless you really need me, I'll bow out."

"I've got a list, so I'll be fine."

"And I suspect that you'd prefer just taking Brandon to trying to drag my four along on the shopping expedition," Samantha said with a grin.

"I love your kids, Samantha, but you're right, one would be easier than five."

"Well, if you change your mind and need help tomorrow or Friday, call," Samantha assured her.

"Oh, wait a minute, I have something else for you two." Carly dug through her huge bag and handed them each an envelope. "I graduate next Wednesday night. I know it's short notice, and graduations are boring, but—"

Before Carly could uninvite them, Michelle said, "I'll be there."

"Me, too," Samantha promised. "You've worked hard for this, and I'll sit in the audience and preen over you. Oh, and I just got a new camera."

Carly groaned. "Really, you don't have to feel as if…" Her sentence faded and she looked at Michelle and Samantha. "No matter what I say, you're both coming, right?"

She tried to look disgruntled, but Michelle could see how much it meant to her.

"Yes," they assured her in unison.

"Will the rest of your family be there?" she asked.

Carly shook her head. "Mom and Dad are in the Bahamas. But my kids will be there. Then they're going to spend the night at their dad's. Maybe we could go out?"

"A girls' night out," Samantha said, rubbing her hands together. "As a mother of four, I need all the nights out I can get."

"We'll just skip our regular meeting next Friday," Carly said.

They'd finished making their plans as Daniel and Harry came back.

"The kids are ready," Daniel announced. "And for the record, I rounded up more than Harry. And here I thought principals were good at intimidating."

"My four know Harry too well to be intimidated, but you're new. Give them a couple days and you'll lose your ability to scare them, as well. Then watch out," Samantha warned Daniel.

The adults gathered their coats and bags. Harry wrapped his arm around Samantha. "The kids bribed me into asking if we could do Patti's for dinner."

"What did they bribe you with?" she asked with a laugh as they walked toward the door.

"Let's see, all four promised to behave and be polite. Stan promised not to hit his younger brothers, Seton promised to eat some salad, Shane wouldn't go that far, but he promised no unnecessary burping, and Stella promised not to set the table on fire."

"Those are impressive bribes, all right. Patti's it is." She turned to her friends. "See you later."

"The door's locked, just make sure you close it behind you," Harry added. He dropped his arm from Samantha's shoulder and took her hand instead. They gathered the kids and left.

"Samantha and Harry," Carly said with a sigh that might have been wistfulness. "Who'd have thought when we got together in September that the two of them would be like that—" she nodded at the doorway they'd just gone through "—in December?"

It was clear she didn't expect an answer, because she didn't even pause before saying, "I'll see you, as well. If you want another craft day, let me know when," Carly said as her kids, Sean and Rhiana, appeared in the doorway, and called to her, "Come on, Mom."

Carly waved and left with them. Which left Daniel and Michelle. She busied herself gathering her things. "Daniel, thanks so much. I suspect making a beanbag toss is closer to your comfort zone than making spiders, and you didn't get to spend much time with Brandon."

"Hey, it turns out I make a mean spider. And I enjoyed getting to know your friends. I liked them. Harry seems like a real down-to-earth guy."

She walked to the door and switched off the lights. "I confess I don't know him well, but he makes Samantha happy and that makes him pretty okay in my book. And your spiders were pretty good."

"So, want to do dinner?"

"Daniel, you don't have to feel as if—"

He cut her off. "I want to. I like spending time with you and Brandon, and as you said, I didn't get to spend much time with him this afternoon. And eating dinner with the two of you sure beats eating all alone."

"I'm glad Chloe wasn't around to hear that. You'd have hurt her feelings." It was lame, and she knew it, but she didn't know what else to say.

"Chloe's good for keeping my feet warm at night, but she's not much for conversation."

Closer and closer. There didn't seem to be any way to maintain her distance from Daniel. And at the moment, Michelle couldn't remember her reasons for wanting to. She knew she had a list, but all she could seem to concentrate on was Daniel's eyes. Dark. So like Brandon's.

She was never able to say no to Brandon when he looked at her with that kind of want, and she was finding it hard to say no to Daniel, as well. "Dinner it is. I've got it all set up at home, if you don't mind eating in, rather than out. I did taco meat up last night, and only have to reheat it and set out the taco fixings."

"Sounds great." He started toward the door, but when she didn't follow, he stopped.

"Daniel, I do worry though. At first it was just for Brandon, and how he's going to feel if you're not his dad. But now, I worry that you're going to get hurt, as well." And if she was honest, she worried about her own feelings. Despite what she'd told her friends, she was beginning to care about Daniel. It was impossible to maintain as much distance as she ought to.

"Thanks for worrying, but, Michelle, even if I'm not Brandon's father, I was his mother's friend. I'm not planning to disappear, no matter how the test comes back, as long as that's all right with you?"

Michelle was saved from answering when Brandon ran up and joined them. "I beat Sean and Seton playing PIG." He paused. "Do you play, Dan?"

"I was on Prep's basketball team, back in the day, and I'm pretty sure I remember how it's done."

"Could we toss the ball a few minutes before we go, Aunt Shell?"

The door was locked, and all they had to do was shut it behind them and she was sure Harry would understand. "I don't mind, if Daniel doesn't?" She ended the sentence as more of a question for Daniel.

"Mind?" Daniel chucked Brandon's shoulder. "I appreciate the opportunity to show him how it's done. Come on, Bran. One quick game of PIG, then your aunt's promised me tacos, if you don't mind my coming to dinner?"

Brandon's grin just about cracked his face. "I don't mind." He turned to Michelle with appreciation in his eyes. "Thanks, Aunt Shell."

"Go shoot your PIG so we can go eat." She shooed them down onto the gym floor. She sat on the stage and watched the two of them shoot around. Daniel set up ridiculous shots. "This one's over the back and to the right," he called as he made his shot backward.

"Wow," Brandon called when Daniel made it.

Michelle liked that Daniel didn't condescend to losing for Brandon's benefit. He beat her nephew fair and square, but didn't gloat as Brandon lost with a PIG to Daniel's PI. He just clapped him on the back. "Good game."

Brandon looked up and said, "I'll beat you next time."

Side by side, they walked toward her. So much alike.

Michelle hadn't seen the similarities at first, but they were there. Brandon was all gangly legs and arms, yet in that ungainliness he had a way of moving that was reminiscent of Daniel. A potential for a shared height and structure there.

But it was more than that. The shape of the eye. Their expressions.

It wasn't so hard to believe they could be father and son.

The thought was a comfort in a way it hadn't been before.

DANIEL HAD BEEN SURPRISED, after his game of PIG with Brandon, when Michelle had offered to let the two of them go pick up Chloe and bring the dog back to her house. She said she'd start dinner.

She'd let him have Brandon on his own before, but it had never been her suggestion. Daniel took it to mean she was finally starting to trust him.

Unlike big cities, where a drive from town to county might take a significant amount of time, it wasn't fifteen minutes to get from the school to Daniel's, and he made even better time heading in to Erie because he was moving in the opposite direction of the after-work traffic.

"Hey, Dan?" Brandon asked from the back seat as they stopped for the red light at the Belle Valley fire station.

Brandon had insisted that Chloe didn't like riding by herself and had joined her, so Daniel was able to glance in the rearview mirror to see the boy. "Yes?"

"Can you tell me about my mom? About the two of you?"

"It will take more than just the five minutes we have left, but sure. Your mom was my best friend. I went to Penn State University, on the main campus in State College. It was a long way from home, and I missed my grandparents, and all my friends here in Erie. Your mom was working at a restaurant I went to, and one day I said something about home, and she asked where it was, and turns out, she was from Erie, too."

"She never liked it here, though," Brandon said.

Daniel noted Brandon's very serious expression.

"I don't think it was that she didn't like Erie, it's just your mom…" He tried to think of a description of Tara. "Your mom was a free spirit. She was so full of life, so filled with a sense of possibility. I don't know that there was any city anywhere that could have held on to her. She was always anxious to see what was around the next bend. She talked about leaving State College practically from the day I met her."

"But she stayed around."

"For a while. She helped me through losing my grandparents. She helped me figure out what I should do with my life. That's a gift, Brandon."

"But she left you. Just like she left all the other guys. She was always sure that her new guy was the one she was looking for, but he never was. Not even you." There was a maturity in Brandon's voice that didn't sound as if it belonged to a seventh-grader.

"Your mom and I were friends. Good friends. And I won't lie, it hurt when she left, but Bran, she never promised me she'd stay. I wasn't angry. Well, at least not for long. Your mom was who she was. Fighting that would be like fighting the wind. There's no sense to it. You can't stay angry at the wind."

"I'm angry that she never told me who my dad was," he admitted. "I used to worry that maybe she didn't want me to know because he wasn't a good guy, but you are. So, why wouldn't she tell me?"

"Maybe she wanted you to live with your aunt. Maybe she was afraid that I'd be mad that she didn't tell me about you. Sometimes I think maybe your mom was afraid of a lot of things."

"What do you mean?" Brandon asked.

When Daniel glanced back this time, the boy was hugging Chloe's head, running his hand through her thick coat.

"Maybe she never told me, never told you because she was afraid I'd insist on being a part of your life…."

"And maybe she wanted to be everything to me?" Brandon asked. "That would make her selfish."

"Or afraid," Daniel pointed out gently. "Afraid she'd lose you."

"Maybe," he admitted. "It's hard to be mad at someone who's gone."

"Yeah, it is."

"Maybe I'll try not to be."

"Me, too." They pulled up at Michelle's. "We can talk more whenever you want. I have lots of stories about your mom. Like right after I met her, some guy at her table patted her rump and called her sweetheart, so she *accidentally* spilled a glass of water on his pants, and said, 'Oh, darling, I'm so sorry.' Rather than be mad, the guy started laughing, and left her a huge tip. That's how your mom was. She could do outrageous stuff, and people wouldn't get mad—"

"They'd tip her."

"Uh-huh."

Brandon opened the house door to the smell of spicy taco meat. Daniel followed him in, leaned down and removed Chloe's lead. She took off, running along the hallway, sniffing everything as she did.

"Oh, man, Dan, smell that? Aunt Shell's tacos are the best. Better than any restaurant's."

Daniel kicked off his shoes, and hung his coat up on a vacant hook. He followed Brandon toward the kitchen and realized he had a hi-honey-I'm-home feeling.

Thinking of the phrase reminded him of his grandparents. It's what his grandfather said every night when he came in from work. That's how the scene played out in Daniel's mind. His grandmother, stirring a huge pot, and his grandfather greeting her and lightly kissing her cheek.

As he walked into the kitchen, Chloe had hurried to the back door and was intent on sniffing what looked to be a pair of Brandon's boots. Michelle wasn't stirring anything. She was carrying a stack of plates to the table. She looked up and smiled as they entered. "Just in time."

Even though she wasn't at the stove, for a moment—just a split second—Daniel could almost imagine himself walking over to her and lightly kissing her cheek.

He shook the feeling off. It was ridiculous. Michelle Hamilton was a nice enough lady, but he'd only known her a little more than a week.

And yet, the feeling remained as the three of them shared another meal. Brandon regaled them with his day at school, and Michelle talked about a new client at work. Then they both focused on him, waiting for him to take a turn sharing his day.

How long had it been since someone had not only asked about his day but cared enough to listen? An enormous lump formed in Daniel's throat. He forced himself to talk around it, praying he sounded natural as he told them about the hundred-plus-year-old banister he was working on. "It's actually in great shape. There are only a couple posts that were damaged, and I'm going to replicate them in the shop."

They all cleaned the kitchen together, which didn't take long. "Homework, Bran," Michelle said.

"Can we take Chloe for a walk first? She likes to walk after dinner, right, Dan?"

"I'm sure she can wait—" he started.

But Michelle interrupted him. "I think Brandon can put his homework off for a bit longer if you two want to take Chloe for her after-dinner walk."

Daniel should have accepted her offer straight out. He knew it was another sign that she was learning to trust him with Brandon, and that thought warmed him. But instead of accepting it, he found himself asking, "Would you join us? I know it's cold, and you're probably tired after working, then the school…"

"I'd love to."

They bundled up in boots and heavy coats, then headed outside.

"You two lead the way," Daniel said. "I don't know the neighborhood that well."

"Why don't we walk to the playground and back," Brandon said.

"Sounds good," Michelle agreed.

It was one of those crisp, clear December nights. There weren't quite as many stars visible in the city as there were in his backyard, but there were enough. The moon was almost full, and looked huge on the horizon.

It was cold enough that he could see Brandon's breath as the boy said, "Dan was telling me about my mom on the drive home, Aunt Shell. Did you know she once spilled water on a guy on purpose 'cause he patted her butt?"

"No," Michelle said slowly. "I didn't, but that sounds like your mom."

"Can you tell us something else, Dan?" Brandon asked.

He tried to catch Michelle's eye to make sure it was okay with her. She gave an almost imperceptible nod, so he said, "Well, as I've said before, your mom had a big heart. There were these three kids who lived somewhere near the restaurant. They used to come in with hands filled with change, count it out and ask her what they could get for it. She'd told me about them long before I ever saw them, and she told me that they didn't look as if they had enough to eat. I was there the day she did it."

"Did what?" Brandon asked, hanging on Daniel's every word.

"She went to their table, and there was just a small pile of change on the edge. She smiled and told them to put it away. 'You all have won,' she told them. 'You're our ten thousandth table served, and that means tonight you win dinner on the house. So, let's start with an appetizer.'"

"Was there really a contest?" Brandon asked.

"No. Your mom paid for their dinner from her tips." He didn't add that he'd split the bill with her. That didn't matter. After what Brandon said about being mad at his mom, he figured the boy needed something nice to hang on to.

"She brought out salads and milk for all three kids. Then hamburgers and fries, and afterward, she served huge sundaes. I stayed the whole time and watched them, listened to them chatter excitedly that they'd won. Your mom gave them that. She spent her own money just because she thought they needed it more than she did. That was your mom. Generous."

"I didn't know that about my mom."

"Your mom had her faults, Brandon. Everyone does. But she had good qualities, too. You just remember those."

"Thanks, Dan."

They were all quiet after that. Three people, walking a dog after dinner on a moonlit December night.

And right at that moment, it was enough.

IT WAS NINE O'CLOCK. Daniel had stuck around after they walked the dog. He'd helped Brandon study for a social studies test, and then they'd all played a game of slapjack.

Brandon was too old to tuck in, but he'd come and kissed Michelle's cheek, then stood in front of Daniel, looking undecided about what to do.

Daniel solved Brandon's dilemma by patting his shoulder. "Thanks for a great night, Bran."

"You're welcome," he said, then darted up the stairs.

"I should probably go now." Daniel got up off the couch.

Michelle rose, as well. "Thanks for giving him that story about Tara. She left and was gone so many years. I can share stories from when we were little, but I didn't ever really have a chance to know her as an adult. I got the occasional call—her just checking on me—but she never shared anything of her life with me when I asked. She never even told me about Brandon."

Michelle had told him that before, but this time—maybe because he knew her better—he could hear the pain in her voice. "I'm sorry."

She added, "I'd have loved to know Brandon as a baby."

"Me, too." He'd tried to imagine what it would have been like if Tara had come to him and told him about Brandon. He'd have offered to marry her. Not just offered, he'd have wanted to. But try as he might, he couldn't imagine Tara would have been happy married to him.

"I tell myself I can't change the past, so I have to appreciate the present. Most of the time I remember, but sometimes?" She shrugged. "It hurts and I get mad all over again, then I feel guilty about being mad at her. She's gone. What can it accomplish?"

"Brandon and I talked about that in the car. He said it's hard to be mad at someone who's gone."

"He's right."

They were both still standing in front of the couch and Daniel realized he really had overstayed his welcome and needed to go, but he found it hard to leave. It wasn't just Brandon. It was Michelle. He liked spending time with her. "Well, I probably should go. *Magellan's Place* starts soon, and I'll confess, I'm addicted."

"Me, too. It's my favorite new show of the year." She glanced at her watch. "You'll never make it home in time. If you want, you can watch it here."

Daniel could tell her that he had a DVR and the show would be waiting for him when he got home. Instead, he simply said, "Thanks. That would be nice. It's been a long time since I had someone to share my love of geek TV with."

Magellan's Place was about Fred Magellan, an adventurer who'd traveled the world and ended up in Place, British Columbia, through a series of mishaps. Place was a sleepy small town with an eclectic, eccentric citizenship that was equal to its town's odd name. "Did you see the episode where Fred and Marshall get stranded…?"

They spent the ten minutes before the show started talking about it, then settled back, side by side on the couch to watch it.

Daniel had missed the simple pleasure of sharing a favorite show with someone. The last time he'd enjoyed this was… He tried to remember. When he dated Kathryn? They'd both been head over heels for *West Wing* in its Shlamme and Sorkin days.

But by the time the producers of the show had changed, they'd lost interest in both the show and each other.

When was that? Sometime in the early 2000s. Oh, he'd dated since, but he'd never had a relationship last long enough to develop a shared favorite show.

"You're quiet," Michelle said, during a commercial.

"Just thinking that it's been a long time since I had this," he admitted.

"This?"

"Someone to enjoy a show with after a long day. It's nice."

"Yes, it is." She seemed hesitant in the response.

"But?" he asked.

"But I don't know how comfortable the two of us should get with each other. I mean, our situation is complicated as it is."

"Well, unfortunately for you, then, I like you."

"I like you, too." She sounded less than pleased at the thought. He laughed. "You don't have to sound so depressed about it."

"Like I said, our situation is complicated enough."

"Well, let's play it out. If the test results come back that I'm not Daniel's father, then you've both gained a friend, and if I am Daniel's father, then you and I liking each other will make my being a part of his life easier, wouldn't you think?"

"We haven't discussed just how you see yourself doing that. Being Brandon's father, if you are. How would you fit into his life?"

Daniel detected that this was a loaded question. "How do you see me fitting in?"

"I'm his legal guardian. I've raised him for the last five years. If you fought me for custody and won, I don't know what I'd do, but I'm pretty sure that would be the end of our liking each other."

"Do you really think I'd do something like that? That I'm

here to tear you and Brandon apart?" He didn't even pause for her to reply. "Because I thought you were starting to trust me. I saw you letting Brandon come back to pick up Chloe with me as a sign that you were getting to know me. But I guess I was wrong."

Her words had cut at him because he wanted Michelle to trust him, to know him. It was important to him in a way that wasn't just about Brandon.

He stood.

She stood, as well, and grabbed his arm. "Daniel, I didn't mean—"

"What, Michelle?" His anger boiled to the surface. "Didn't mean to imply that I'm the kind of man who would rip the only stable home his son has ever known out from under him? Brandon told me something about how it was, moving around with Tara. He told me how much he loves knowing he'll sleep in his own bed, in his own room each night. You gave him that. Do you really think I'm the kind of man who would try to worm his way into your good graces just so I can sue you for custody later and take him from you?"

"I'm sorry. I shouldn't have implied…" She paused. "Daniel, even though I do like you and I do trust you with Brandon, the truth is we've only known each other a short time. I don't think you would ever try to rip Brandon away from me, but can you really blame me for worrying? I've trusted people in the past, and had them let me down. I know I can't let those times color the rest of my life, but it's hard. The heart's not as resilient as the head thinks it should be."

He wanted to stay mad at her, but he knew if Brandon was his and someone came into his life, he'd be as cautious as Michelle. "You're right. I'd worry if the tables were turned. And to be honest, I haven't figured out how you and I will make it work, but we'll do it together. We both want what's best for Brandon. We're both reasonable people. And since we both love *Magellan's Place,* we obviously have a great deal of taste and insight."

She smiled at that, which had been his intent. "I still maintain liking each other isn't another complication. And even if it is, I can't just stop liking you because you think it would be more convenient."

"Me, either." She stood on tiptoes and kissed his cheek, just the slightest peck. "You're very easy to like, Daniel McLean, darn it all."

He smiled and leaned down and kissed her on the cheek as well. "You, too, Michelle Hamilton."

Two platonic cheek kisses.

That's all they'd been.

Just two small busses that were less than a European double-cheek greeting by half. That's all there should have been.

But it wasn't.

That slight contact lit an attraction for Michelle that Daniel hadn't realized was there. He'd known he liked her. Realized that she was a pretty lady. But he hadn't realized there was more to it than that until now.

He leaned down to kiss her again, nothing impersonal at all about it this time. As a matter of fact, this kiss was as personal as he could make it. His lips against hers, soft and pliant. The kiss grew deeper, with Michelle participating wholeheartedly. Then, abruptly, she pulled back. "Daniel, we—"

He didn't want to let her go, but he did. He moved back a step and sighed. "I know, I know. Complications and all that."

She shot him a rueful smile. "Yes."

"Fine. We won't. But there's something between us, Michelle. Something that seems to be growing at a rapid pace."

"Something we can't afford to let continue," she said softly. "Maybe you should go." She took half a step as if to herd him toward the front door.

He didn't budge. "If I sit back down on the far end of the couch and promise to keep a whole cushion between us, could I stay until the end of *Magellan's Place?* You wouldn't want me to miss any."

"Fine. You stay on your end, I'll stay on mine." She sat as close to the end of the couch as she could get and not be sitting on the arm. "If Chloe wasn't in sleeping with Brandon, I'd put her on the middle cushion."

"Because you can't trust yourself. Yes, I know, I have that effect on women. I try not to, but…" he teased and sat, as well.

The teasing lightened the mood a bit, as the commercial ended and Fred Magellan was back on the small screen. From all appearances, Michelle had forgotten all about their kiss and fallen back into the show.

Unfortunately, it wasn't that easy for Daniel.

He was pretty sure he wouldn't be forgetting that particular kiss for some time to come.

When the show's credits rolled, and scenes from next week's episode came on, Daniel stood up. "I should really go this time. It feels like I've been standing next to this couch and saying that all night."

She nodded, so he continued, "I think Chloe's still in with Brandon. Do you mind if I get her?"

"Sure."

He led the way up the stairs to Brandon's room. The door was ajar. He peeked inside and Chloe was curled at the end of the bed, her head resting on Brandon's legs. Her tail made a tired wag as she spotted him, but she didn't even lift her head.

Daniel wasn't sure how to get her out without waking

Brandon. Soon, he didn't worry about it, as he studied the boy's face all in shadows from the weak light from the hall. And he wondered if Tara had done this—stood in the hall, looking in on Brandon as he slept. Had she gone in and covered him when he was little and kicked off his covers? Had she kept a night-light on for him?

"I do it, too," Michelle said softly from behind him.

"What?" he whispered back.

"Watch him sleep. When he first came here, I'd check in many times every night because he'd been so broken up about Tara's passing and he didn't know me well enough to come to me then for comfort. He'd soldier through the day. But at night, he'd cry in his room. This little bit of a boy who'd lost everything he'd ever known, crying by himself. It broke me, Daniel."

He wanted to reach out and put his arm around her, pull her to him, but he knew she wouldn't welcome the gesture, so he simply kept his distance. "You helped him through it."

"It wasn't easy. I had a lot to learn, and he was so confused. The first year was hard." She stopped. "Sorry, you needed to get going."

He wasn't sorry. He wished she'd kept talking, kept sharing. But he didn't push. He nodded to the dog. "I'm afraid I'm going to wake Brandon up if I go in and get her."

"She can spend the night," Michelle offered. "I can drop her off at your place in the morning after I drop Brandon off at school."

Her offer surprised him, but maybe it shouldn't. Michelle had proved to be very considerate and generous. "Are you sure?"

"Brandon will be thrilled to wake up and find her here, as long as you don't mind."

"I don't. Thanks."

They went back down the stairs, and he half expected

Chloe to come down on her own, but she evidently was content with Brandon.

"I'll see you in the morning then." Again, he was consumed by the need to pull her into his arms and kiss her good-night. But Michelle's body language was as good as if she were screaming no. One arm was folded across her chest, and she stood partially behind the door, gripping the handle with her other hand, as if she needed to be able to close the door on him and escape at a moment's notice.

"Yes, I'll see you in the morning," she repeated. "Thanks for tonight."

He left and heard Michelle shut the door, and he glanced behind him.

Since he'd bought his cottage in Greene Township, he'd always looked forward to going home at night. But tonight, going home didn't provide him the normal rush of satisfaction because he recognized that the cottage was merely a house. Michelle's was a home—one he wished he didn't have to leave.

Chapter Eight

Saturday morning, Daniel offered to pick Michelle and Brandon up on his way into town so they could go to the dollar store before skating.

Michelle had successfully avoided being alone with him on Thursday and Friday, but she hadn't been able to think of a way to gracefully say no to his suggestion—at least not one that Brandon would buy. Which was why she was sitting in the front seat of his truck Saturday morning, while Brandon sat in the back, wearing his iPod.

"You're awfully quiet," Daniel said as they drove across East Thirty-Eighth to the dollar store.

"Sometimes quiet is good." She'd been afraid he'd want to talk. She'd hoped Brandon's presence would delay the discussion, but thanks to technology, Brandon was present but not listening.

"And sometimes too quiet means there's a problem." Daniel glanced her way. "And it seems to me our problems began Wednesday night when we—"

She cut him off in case Brandon could hear over the iPod buds in his ears. "We had a lovely time yesterday, I thought. I hadn't noticed any problems, other than I can't punch a tin lid as well as you can.'"

He cocked his head and just gave her a look, before turning his attention to the road. "I noticed you had Brandon tell me that you canceled our shopping trip when *he* dropped off Chloe on Thursday morning. And instead of the three of us shopping, we made more crafts with Samantha and Carly. They both even went so far as to invite us all out to dinner. Thursday night, Samantha, then Friday night, Carly. We haven't been alone once since *Magellan's Place* on Wednesday."

She tried to look confused on the off chance that he glanced her way again. He didn't. He kept his eyes on the road, and both hands on the steering wheel. "They're good friends and wanted to help. That's why I put off the shopping until this morning. It made sense since we were going skating anyway. No other reason. Certainly not because of a problem. And we haven't been alone because…" She paused a moment, thinking. The truth was they hadn't been alone because she'd done a good job of making sure they weren't. Although she wasn't going to tell him the truth. Instead, she finished, "…because things have been busy, in case you hadn't noticed."

"Uh-huh." It was only two syllables of agreement, but he managed to infuse them with a sarcastic lilt that made them more of a negative than a positive.

"What's that supposed to mean?"

"I think it means something about Wednesday made you nervous. I don't think it was our discussion, or even watching *Magellan's Place* together." He paused. "Gee, what could it be that would make you nervous enough to cancel our solo shopping trip and call in crafting reinforcements?"

She checked on Brandon, who still seemed absorbed in whatever was playing on his iPod. "I suggest this conversation is best left to another, more private time."

"I just thought that if I told you that if you-know-what-we're-talking-about is what's making you nervous, I'll simply promise to see that it doesn't happen again."

She was about to say yes, that would be good, when he added, "Can you make the same promise?"

"What do you mean, can I? Of course I can. It's not like you're that irresistible." That was a lie and she knew it. The idea of kissing him was tempting, even now, as he teased her.

"I don't know. You seemed to have trouble resisting Wednesday." He shot her a rather amused smile.

Michelle was not finding the conversation amusing in the least. "I'll figure something out," she promised him.

His amusement was even more evident. "I'm sure you will."

"Hey, what did I miss?" Brandon asked from the back as he took the earbuds out.

"Nothing worth mentioning," Michelle said stiffly.

They made short work of the dollar store and left with three giant bags stuffed with coloring books, crayons, hair paraphernalia and other small items that the children who shopped at the Christmas Fair could give to their families as gifts, then hurried to the skating rink on West Thirty-Eighth Street.

Michelle rented her skates and arrived at the bleachers to find Brandon was already out on the ice. Daniel was waiting for her. "Want help lacing your skates? I've heard that in the day, it was not only considered chivalrous, but also allowed a gentleman the opportunity to catch a glimpse of the lady's ankle. Very risqué at the time."

"Well, these days, women are self-sufficient and lace their own skates," she informed him as primly as possible. "Rumor has it most gentlemen don't find ankles all that risqué anymore."

Then, as she laced and tightened her boot, Daniel's thigh brushed against hers. There was a sudden race of her heart reminding her all over again and she pulled back.

"Do I really make you that uncomfortable?" Daniel asked softly.

"No, you don't make me uncomfortable. My actions on Wednesday night make me uncomfortable. We've only known each other a week and a half. And even without stopping to consider the situation…even without that, I don't normally go around kissing men I've only known a week and a half."

"I don't think there's anything normal about our entire situation. I've spent more time with you in the past week than I've spent with women I've dated for months. Maybe that's why I don't feel weirded out by the scant amount of time we've known each other."

He was right. She'd dated men much longer, and hadn't managed to rack up as many hours in their company as she had with Daniel.

Even Samantha and Carly. She'd known them in a peripheral way before their committee was formed in September. But over the last three months they'd gone from acquaintances to true friends. The three of them had just clicked. Time hadn't been an issue.

She didn't have an argument for him. She simply said, "Well, I do feel uncomfortable, and I'd like to keep our distance."

"So you called in your cavalry to act as buffers."

"I was thinking chaperones, but buffer is also an apt description."

"Because you're afraid you can't keep your hands off me." He shook his head in mock disapproval. "Really, Michelle, you need to learn self-restraint."

"I am the queen of self-restraint. I guarantee that I can keep my hands off you."

"So prove it. Spend the rest of the day with Brandon and me and don't kiss me. I promise I won't kiss you."

"As if I'd let you." With her skates dutifully laced, she got up and headed for the rink, Daniel at her heels. "It's not going to happen, Daniel."

"If you say so."

Brandon skated up to them. "Want to see what I learned, Aunt Shell?"

"Sure." He'd been coming almost weekly to the rink with friends. She hoped that today's excursion wasn't going to start another round of hockey-league pleas.

Michelle was a step-above-the-basics skater. She could do laps around the rink, but things like going backward, or even stopping, could throw her for a loop.

Brandon, on the other hand, was going full throttle, passing her more than once, switching from skating forward to skating backward, stopping on a dime, then speeding right back up.

"He's good," Daniel said.

"Yes," she agreed. Most of the time Brandon excelling at anything left her feeling nothing but pride. However, a contact sport left her feeling only trepidation. She didn't want him playing hockey, but watching him on the ice, she could see he was in his element here, and he'd probably be a natural at the sport, which left her feeling guilty for saying no.

Since when was loving someone enough to want to keep them safe a crime?

But that's how it felt. As if, in this instance, she wasn't thinking so much of keeping Brandon safe, as she was thinking about keeping herself from worrying.

She thought about it as they skated. Brandon met up with a group of friends, and Daniel and Michelle ended up at the refreshment stand ordering hot chocolates.

"So, dinner tonight?" Daniel asked as they snagged a table. "I have a roast in the Crock-Pot, unless you're afraid to be alone with me. If that's the case, we could go to a very public restaurant and get something there."

"I'm glad you're finding this amusing."

"I'm not…not really. Though we seem to be going in circles, so let's call a truce. Come on over and have dinner with me tonight."

"Okay." There was no hope for it. She was going to prove to Daniel—and maybe to herself—that this attraction wasn't a big deal.

She could handle it.

DANIEL COULDN'T REMEMBER when he'd had so much fun. Michelle had sat out awhile, leaving him some private time with Brandon on the ice. The kid was good. Very good.

When they'd finished, they'd all headed back to his place. He'd let Michelle and Brandon in, then walked out to the street to get the mail, hoping against all hope that the paternity test results had been returned. Doing so had become part of his daily ritual.

He was still thumbing through his mail when he entered the kitchen and found Michelle sitting alone at the counter. "Bran took Chloe outside?"

"They're in the back. Should I call them in?"

"No, give me a minute to get things ready. I'm sure he's having fun with Chloe, and she loves having someone whose energy level is as unflagging as her own."

Daniel hurriedly finished going through the mail, disappointed but not surprised that the results weren't there.

"Nothing yet?" she asked softly.

He looked up from the pile of mail.

"You were checking for the results, right?" she asked.

"Yes. Nothing again today."

"I started looking the day after you two had the tests done, even though I knew that there was no way the results would arrive that soon. Every day I go to the mailbox and get this sick feeling in the pit of my stomach."

"You're sick at the thought that I'm Brandon's father?"

"No," she said. "At first I was, but now? I'm sick at the thought that you're not his father."

He whirled her around and, despite his good intentions, he kissed her. He'd forgotten all about his promise. Even if he'd remembered, he'd probably have still done it. "Thanks for that."

"I thought we agreed you wouldn't kiss me?" she asked, sounding flustered, as she moved away and smoothed imaginary wrinkles from her sweater.

"That was a peck on the cheek, not a real kiss. It was a thanks for hoping that I'm Brandon's dad. That matters to me."

"We still haven't worked out what it will mean. We've spent the past week and a half living in each other's back pocket, but that can't go on. Tax season will be starting, which means long days for me. I'll be back to working until five. We won't be spending every day together like this, although I know you'll still want to be with Brandon."

"Not just Brandon," Daniel admitted. It was true. He saw Brandon and Michelle as a package. A family. He didn't want to just be Brandon's father, he wanted to be part of their family. He didn't know how to word it. "Your allowing me to spend time with Brandon has been a gift. No matter what, I don't want to lose him from my life. But I don't want to lose you, either."

"Daniel—"

She didn't finish her sentence, because Brandon and Chloe charged in the back door. "Time to eat yet? I'm starving."

Michelle seemed relieved to see him. "He's grown inches

since the end of last year. But I still don't know where he puts all the food he manages to eat."

"Hollow foot," Brandon teased. "It all sinks right down to my hollow foot. And right now, me and the foot are starving."

"Well, we don't want that." Daniel started pulling the roast from the Crock-Pot and tried not to let his disappointment show. He'd wanted Michelle to finish her statement. He wanted things worked out. But it was probably best that Brandon had come in, because he suspected Michelle would simply pull back further if he kept pushing. Even that small peck on the cheek had startled her. Reining in his emotions was hard. He hadn't exactly sorted them out, but he did know that he wanted both Michelle and Brandon in his life.

Michelle and Brandon had set the table by the time he brought the roast and side dishes over.

"We make quite a team," he told them both.

They sat down and Brandon burst out, "Oh, Aunt Shell, Sean wanted to know if I could come over tomorrow.…"

Daniel listened to Brandon's excited talk about going to his friend's. A feeling of familiar swept over him. A delightful feeling. These meals, shared with Brandon and Michelle, were starting to be the highlight of Daniel's day.

They cleared the table after they finished and Daniel started washing the dishes, while Michelle packaged up the leftovers.

Brandon dried and set the dishes on the counter. "Hey, Dan, how's that desk thing coming that you were working on?"

"Do you want to go out and see when we're done?"

Brandon looked to his aunt for permission.

Michelle nodded and walked over and took the towel from him. "Why don't you two go do that? I'll finish drying the dishes."

"Why don't you just let the dishes drip and come out with us?" Daniel asked.

"Aunt Shell doesn't do drip-dry dishes." Brandon laughed and dodged as Michelle swatted him with the towel.

Daniel loved seeing the connection between the two of them. They were a unit. He could understand Michelle's initial concerns. She didn't want anyone hurting what the two of them had built. He got that.

He hoped she was beginning to see that he didn't want to destroy their relationship. He wanted to be a part of it. He wanted to be able to tease her the way Brandon did. He wanted Brandon to give him those looks that asked for permission, or asked his opinion.

He wanted to be part of their family.

It had been a long time since he belonged somewhere. The thought came unbidden, and made Daniel feel like an interloper.

"You two go have some man-bonding time," Michelle insisted.

They hadn't even reached the workshop when Brandon said, "So did you see me skating this afternoon?"

There was an intensity in the question that warned Daniel that this trip to the shed was about something more than seeing his progress on the secretary. "Yes, you were great."

"I know." He grinned. "It's a curse." Brandon turned serious. "But now you see why I want to try out for the hockey team. I'm kind of old, and I know it, but I'm a good skater, and I understand the game, so I think I could make it. I just need Aunt Shell to see it."

"Maybe she'll change her mind."

Brandon shook his head. "Aunt Shell is great, but when she comes to a decision, there's not much that will shake her. Although maybe if you talk to her, she might."

Daniel could see the potential minefield this could easily become. "Brandon, I don't think I should interfere."

"My mom always talked about following her dreams. That dreams were important, 'cause without them what was the point? Well, this is my dream, Dan. I can't just ignore Aunt Shell and go after it myself. I'm too young. And by the time I'm old enough to do what I want, I'll be too old. But you could talk to her. You could make her see that this is my dream, that she should let me go after it. I might not make it, but I'll never know if I don't at least try."

"Bran—"

"Please?"

There was such hope in Brandon's eyes. A sense of surety that if Daniel talked to Michelle, he could get her to change her mind. He could help Brandon go after his dream.

He'd seen the boy on the ice today, and he was a natural. Daniel was a competent skater at best. Michelle was even more hesitant on the ice than he was. But Brandon? He owned the ice, skating with grace.

"I can't promise anything, but I'll mention it to her. Your aunt has the final word though."

"Great. I know she'll listen to you." Brandon didn't seem to hear anything but the fact Daniel said he'd talk to Michelle.

Daniel wasn't sure how to approach it, but he didn't have time to think it through. Brandon was rushing into the shop. "Can you tell me how you fixed this?" Brandon asked.

Daniel talked him through the process, step by step. "Are you sure this isn't boring you to tears?"

"Nah. I was kinda wondering if maybe…" Brandon paused, as if unsure how to ask his question. "Well, you said your grandfather showed you how to work with wood. He taught you all about the tools and how to use them."

"Yes, he did." Daniel could still remember walking into his grandfather's shop for the first time. He remembered learning what a Phillips head was, what a router did. What had been so alien that first time had quickly become the place he felt most at home. "But he wanted it to be just a hobby. It was your mom who taught me to try to make carpentry my job."

"She helped you?"

"A lot. Your mom was a very good friend. My grandfather didn't mean to, but he gave me the dream and your mom taught me to follow it."

"Well, I wondered if maybe you'd teach me carpentry."

There was a vulnerability in his expression that tugged at Daniel's heart.

Before he could reply, Brandon hurriedly continued, "I know we don't know if you're, like, really my father yet, but even if you're not, I thought maybe I could come out to the shop sometimes and help. I mean, I'd sweep floors or sand stuff. Easy stuff that might help you out, if you'd show me how it all works."

As if to prove he could be of some use, or maybe because he didn't want to look at Daniel in case he said no, Brandon straightened a jumble of screwdrivers on the workbench.

Daniel reached out and gently put his hand on Brandon's, stilling it. "We'd have to clear it with your aunt, but as long as it's okay with her, I'd love to have an apprentice."

Brandon looked up and smiled. "An apprentice? We studied that in social studies. It sounds sort of cool."

"Come on, we'd better get back in before your aunt cleans my whole house. We can ask her about you spending some time in the shop with me." They went outside and Daniel secured the door.

"Aunt Shell does like things neat. And by *like,* I mean, has to have everything neat." Brandon then added, "I don't want you to think she's mean about it or anything. I just like to tease her."

Daniel could see apprehension in Brandon's eyes. The boy didn't want him thinking badly of Michelle. He put a hand on his shoulder. "Brandon, I can tell that you two have a great relationship. If I'd known I was your father and had a choice in who helped raise you, I couldn't think of anyone in the world who'd have done a better job than your aunt."

"If you were my dad and you knew about me, would you have let someone else raise me?"

"Brandon, if I'd known about you, I'd have moved heaven and earth to be a part of your life. I'd have never given you to someone else, but I'd never have tried to take you away from your mom or aunt. And if the test comes back that I am your dad, whatever we do, I'll never take you from your aunt. I'm hoping she'll share you with me. I want to be a part of your life…no matter what any test shows or doesn't show."

"Thanks. Me, too."

Daniel slung his arm around Brandon's shoulder. It was a casual gesture. One his grandfather had done countless times, yet there was nothing casual about it for Daniel. This boy— this amazing boy—might be his son, and this was the first time he'd ever done something as basic as put an arm around him.

He was hit suddenly by the enormity of the things he'd missed. A first step, a first smile. Brandon's first day of school.

It wasn't just all the firsts that he'd missed. He'd missed just listening to Brandon's day. Advising him.

Everything had happened so fast he hadn't really processed the situation. Now, the simple gesture of an arm around Brandon's shoulder brought it truly home.

He'd missed thirteen years. All the basic dad stuff. Teaching Brandon to ride a bike. Playing tooth fairy and Santa for him. Dyeing Easter eggs.

His friend Bob had a two-year-old and had brought him to

the site the other day dressed in Carhartt work pants. Daniel had never had the opportunity to dress his baby in cute clothes. And he couldn't imagine that Brandon would be open to the idea now.

He'd thought he was over being angry at Tara, but maybe he wasn't quite as done as he'd thought. A whole new wave of bitterness swept over him.

They reached the back door. "Dan, you okay? You got real quiet."

He realized he still had his arm over Brandon's shoulder. He took it off and mussed Brandon's hair with it. "I'm fine. I was thinking about how much I wish I'd been able to be around when you were little."

"When I first came to live with Aunt Shell I was…well, I wasn't easy. I was mad and I really hurt 'cause Mom was dying. Then one day Aunt Shell came into my room. She knelt by my bed and said, 'Brandon, we can't change the past. Even if we could, I don't know how we'd change it without making you someone other than who you are. And who you are is pretty fantastic. So, you take as long as you need because you're worth the wait. You and me, we just need to figure out where we go from here.'" He looked at Daniel, his expression so much more mature than it should be. "We can't change the past, Dan. I hope you're my dad, but we'll have to wait and see. But if you are, we'll just have to figure out where we go from here."

"We'll figure it out," Daniel promised as he opened the door. He glanced at Brandon and was totally in awe.

"Don't forget hockey," Brandon whispered.

He looked up at Michelle as they walked into the kitchen, her words that Brandon had shared with him still hanging thick between them.

She smiled at them.

"Dishes are done and we should be heading home. Brandon

has homework to do. If he does it tonight, then he's got tomorrow all clear to go to Sean's." She folded up the dish towel that was still in her hand.

"No problem, Aunt Shell. Why don't I take my stuff out to the car and you and Dan can talk about…whatever."

He grabbed his book bag and coat, patted Chloe goodbye and raced out of the kitchen. Daniel heard the front door close.

Michelle looked at Daniel. "What was that all about?"

"That was Brandon being subtle."

She set the dish towel down on the counter. "Brandon has all the subtlety of an ox in a china shop. So what was he trying to be subtle about?"

"He wanted to give me time to talk to you."

Michelle's expression went from amused to guarded in the blink of an eye. "He wanted you to talk to me about…?"

"Well, we talked about him helping out in the shop after Christmas. I know that power tools are dangerous, so I'd start him out with things like sanding, and hand tools. It would be something we could do together. I learned from my grandfather, and I'd love to pass some of that down to Brandon."

"We're not even sure he's your son." Confusion gave way to wariness.

Daniel had thought they were beyond that. He thought she understood him. He beat down his annoyance. "And I'm hoping he is my son. But even if he isn't, do you think I'd walk away now and say, hey, it was nice meeting you? I like him. I like you. I like having both of you around and, no matter what the paternity test shows, I'd like to be a part of his life, if you'll let me."

He wanted to say that he wanted to be part of both their lives; he wanted to mention their kiss, and say he'd like to think there would be more of those in their future. But Michelle's expression didn't bode well for that conversation, so he let it go for now.

Wary, he added, "Brandon also wanted me to talk to you about his skating. About him being allowed to try out for hockey."

If anything, Michelle looked even more distant. "He's already asked, and I've already given my answer."

"He was hoping I could change your mind. I—" He didn't get to finish his pitch about just offering another opinion because the normally calm, placid Michelle exploded.

"It's starting already, isn't it? You don't know if you're Brandon's father for sure, and yet you feel that after a week and a half you know what's best for him and you can throw your weight around."

"Michelle, that's not it at all," he hastily assured her. "He asked for my help and I told him I'd talk to you, but I didn't promise anything. I didn't say I'd overrule you or try to force the issue. He just wanted me to give you my input."

"And just what input is that, Daniel?"

He should apologize and drop the subject. Michelle was right—he wasn't sure he was Brandon's father. He had no rights. Yet he could see Brandon's face, the yearning in it, and found himself saying, "You should reconsider."

"Ah, a not-for-sure-father for a couple weeks makes you an expert on what Brandon should or shouldn't do?" she asked.

He'd never seen this side of Michelle. He'd only met quiet Michelle of lists and logic. "No, but I know what it's like to want something and have someone tell you no. To put their own vision of the way things should be above yours."

"And that's what I'm doing? That's how you see it?"

"I know you care about him, and that you're worried, but there's no way to make life a hundred percent safe. Tara taught me about going after a dream. This is Brandon's dream. You have to allow him—"

"I have to put aside my worry and allow him?" She laughed, not a normal joy-filled Michelle-sounding laugh, but something tight and pain filled. "You don't know the first thing about worrying about Brandon, Daniel. When he first came to me, that's when I learned what it meant to worry. I worried about every cough and sniffle. I worried that he didn't cry after Tara died. I forced him to go talk to a psychiatrist, then I worried that I was making too much of it and probably had psychologically scarred him by trying to make sure he wasn't psychologically scarred. The worries never go away. I worry about bullies and drugs at school. I worry about having enough money set aside to pay for his college. I'm a queen of worrying, Daniel. And you think I need to add another worry to my rather impressive list? You think I need to see him skate out onto that rink knowing how many ways he could be injured playing a game? Do you really think I need that?"

He should stop. He knew it. But the naked longing he'd seen in Brandon's eyes pushed him to be brutally honest. "What I think is that your last statement says it all. You're saying no to Brandon so *you* won't have to worry, not because you think saying no is what's best for him."

"I—" She stopped and didn't say anything more.

The silence weighed heavily between them and finally Daniel said, "I know you want me to butt out. I don't blame you. However, this decision shouldn't be about your worries. It shouldn't be about you. This isn't me trying to take over. It's me offering another opinion. It's me saying that this decision should be about Brandon growing up and discovering what he wants, even if it means you have to worry because of it."

She didn't argue. She didn't agree. "I have to go," she

said, and hurried to the front door, not even pausing to put her coat on. She just carried it with her as she opened the door.

Daniel followed her. "Michelle, stay and talk this out with me."

She whirled around. "You've made your position very clear, Daniel. Let me make mine equally clear. I am Brandon's guardian. I make decisions on his behalf until he's old enough to make them for himself. You're not even sure you're his father yet. And if the test proves that you are…" She paused. "Well, if it does, we're going to have to come to some terms. But for now, back off. You might not agree with my decisions, still, you're going to have to live with them and so is he."

"Michelle, I don't want to fight."

"There's nothing to fight about. I'm going. I think we should take a break tomorrow. We've been seeing too much of each other since this started. He's going to Sean's, anyway, and I need a day off. I need to think."

"Can I still come help with the Christmas Fair preparations on Monday?" He was afraid she'd say no.

She turned around. "There's no school on Monday and we don't have that much left to finish."

"Tuesday then?" he pressed.

Michelle's expression said she wanted to say no to that, as well, but in the end, she nodded. "If you want."

"Fine. Tell Brandon I'll see him then."

He stood at the front door and watched her dash to her little orange car. Brandon was waiting in it. When she opened her door and the interior light flashed on, Brandon waved to Daniel, and he waved back.

He watched until the car backed out of the driveway and finally moved out of sight.

He'd made a total mess of that.

"Aunt Shell..." Brandon started as soon as Michelle began driving away from Daniel's.

Michelle's emotions were still in a knot and she knew she needed to calm down before they had this particular discussion. "We need to talk, Brandon, but first I need to collect myself, so let's make the ride home in silence."

"But—"

"Brandon, when we get home." She glanced over and he gave her a frustrated look.

Well, that was fine with her, because she was feeling a bit frustrated herself. She prided herself on being open to someone else's opinion, especially when it came to Brandon. Despite the books she'd read, she wasn't anywhere close to being an expert on child rearing. And now that Brandon was a teen, she was even less of an expert.

But when Daniel tried talking to her, she'd gotten completely defensive.

And it wasn't that he was offering a different opinion than hers. It was fear, pure and simple. The same fear that had been gnawing at her since Daniel McLean had shown up on her doorstep. The fear that she was going to lose Brandon.

Daniel wasn't the bad guy.

It would be easier on her if he was. If he'd walked away from Tara and Brandon, Michelle would have an excuse to insulate her nephew from this man.

Easier on *her.*

Just having the thought made her feel guilty. Daniel was right, she was selfish.

He wasn't the kind of man who would have walked away from Tara. He'd never take the easy way out. He'd been working so hard to do what was right since Brandon showed up on his porch. When Brandon had dropped the bombshell,

Daniel hadn't balked. He'd taken the paternity test, and now, even before he was sure Brandon was his, he was taking responsibility, getting to know him.

She felt worse and worse with each mile that passed.

They got home and she'd barely had a chance to hang up her coat before Brandon said, "Now?"

She sighed. "Yes." She walked into the living room and sat on the couch, patting the cushion next to hers.

Reluctantly, Brandon sat next to her. "You're mad."

"I'm…" She wanted to deny she was angry, but she was. She might know it was irrational, that her anger didn't make sense, but it was there, roiling about, an acid in the pit of her stomach. "Not at you."

"At Dan? 'Cause I asked him to talk to you about hockey? He didn't want to. But I needed someone on my side, Aunt Shell. I needed you to see and I didn't know how to tell you."

"No, I'm not mad at Daniel. At least not really. Although, I'm going to tell you up front—before we know for sure if Daniel's your father—that we're not to play that game."

Brandon looked confused. "What game?"

"The one where you think you can get your way in a situation by playing Daniel and myself off against each other."

"That's what you think?" Brandon sprang from the couch and stalked to the end of it, then came back and sat down. "That's what you think? That I'm playing some game? I'll tell you what I was doing. I was trying to find some grown-up to talk to you, to get you to hear me. I thought about asking Mrs. Lewis or Mrs. Williams, but then you and Dan seemed to be getting along, and I thought maybe he could make you listen to me."

She was shocked that Brandon seemed to think he needed assistance in talking to her. "Bran, I always try to listen—"

He interrupted her. "You listen when you want to. But once you've made up your mind about something, you stop hearing me. And, Aunt Shell, you made your mind up about hockey and nothing I said was gonna change it. I thought maybe Dan could talk to you, but I shoulda known better. It doesn't matter what I want. I'm sure when it comes to going to college, you're going to be like Dan's grandfather and try to make me take business classes, or maybe you'll make me be an accountant like you."

"Bran, you can be whatever you want to be," Michelle said.

"That's what you always tell me, but that's a lie. What you really mean is I can be whatever you allow me to be, whatever you think I should be. There's a difference. A big difference, Aunt Shell."

The vehemence in his words shocked her. "Bran—"

"It's true. I guess that's how it works for everyone. People tell you that you can be anything you want, but they don't mean it. Dan's grandfather told him that he had to take business in college, even though Dan wanted to be a carpenter like his grandfather, and anyone can see that's what he's supposed to be. Well, maybe I'd have tried hockey and hated it, but maybe I'd have found that it's what I'm meant to be."

"There's more to you than hockey."

"Yeah? Well, there was more to you than just *the good sister,* but that's what your mom wanted you to be. That's what she told you you were." His voice softened and he suddenly sounded so much older than thirteen. "You were *the good sister,* my mom was the bad sister, the one that always got in trouble—that's what Mom told me. Maybe it's true. Mom always did get in trouble. But maybe it's because she believed her mom. Maybe if my grandmother hadn't said that to her all those years ago, she'd have been different. But Mom believed her mom…your mom. Mom always believed what other people told her. She believed that she was the bad sister, just like she believed all the guys who said they loved her, even when they didn't."

Michelle didn't know what to say to that. There was truth in it. Her mother had never been kind to Tara. She hadn't been overly kind to Michelle, either, but since Michelle didn't rock the boat, they'd had less friction, but they'd certainly never had a close relationship. Not the kind of mother-daughter relationship she'd always dreamed of having.

"Maybe I'd try hockey and hate it, but maybe I wouldn't. You shouldn't try to tell me who I am, and what I should do."

"I shouldn't try to define you," she said, more to herself than him.

Brandon nodded. "Maybe hockey's what I'm meant to do. Just like Daniel found what he was meant to do, even though his grandfather tried to stop him." He paused. "And like you found what you were meant to do."

"Me? Bran, I like my job, but I don't think it's a calling, it's nothing like Daniel's carpentry." She was good at her job—she'd always clicked with numbers—but there was no passion in it for her. It was nothing like what she saw in Brandon's eyes when he tried to coerce her into allowing him to play hockey. Nothing like what she saw when Daniel touched a piece of wood.

"No, not your job, Aunt Shell. Me. You were meant to be a mother to me. Mom loved me, I know that, but she was always so lost, always looking for herself, that she never really saw me. She never did mother sorts of things like worrying about bedtimes and vitamins and stuff. She'd have let me do hockey without worrying that I'd take a puck to the head. Mom worried about herself and her next boyfriend. She was so busy worrying about herself that there wasn't anything left over for me. But then she brought me here."

Michelle could feel tears welling in her eyes.

"I've been thinking about this for a long time," he said, answering her unasked question. "I never had a home till I moved here with you. And I never really knew what a mother should be until you. I loved Mom and she loved me, but she just couldn't do mom stuff. You might be my aunt Shell, but you're the only real mother I've ever known."

"Oh, Bran." And though she knew he felt he was too old for the mushy stuff, she hugged him and held him tight. "I do love you."

"Yeah, I know. Even when I'm mad at you, I know." He hugged her back, but after a second it proved to be more emotion than he could stand and he started to squirm.

She let him go and looked at him. Really looked at this gift. His insight had caught her off guard, but it shouldn't have. He was so smart. He was someone who knew what he wanted and went after it without hesitation. He'd wanted to know his father, and he'd gone after Daniel and found him. Now, he wanted hockey. She'd probably worry every minute he was on the ice, but he was right, he should be allowed to try it.

"Brandon, you are what I was meant to do. I still don't want to say yes about hockey, but—"

Before she could tell him that he could try out, he said, "Then I'll convince you on my own. I have a list. And you know how much you like lists. Well-organized arguments always impress you."

"So, you think you have me figured out?" She smiled, knowing it was watery at best.

"Oh, sure." He grinned. And just like that, their fight was over. "I have my top ten reasons why I should be allowed to play hockey. All logical and sincere. That will convince you."

"Get me your list, and then we'll talk about it. Really talk about it," she assured him. "I'll listen."

But they didn't need to, really. She knew what her answer had to be.

He started out of the room but turned at the doorway. "And you'll make up with Dan?"

She nodded. "I'll apologize for overreacting. The rest will be up to him."

"Good. 'Cause I like him, Aunt Shell. When I started looking, I was realistic. I might have been little, but I remember the guys mom usually hung out with. There were a couple nice ones, but mainly, they weren't so much. Dan's one of the good ones."

Michelle knew Brandon was right. Daniel wasn't just good when compared to the type of guy Tara usually dated. He was just a good one, period. "You're right, he is."

"So are you going to call him?"

"Some apologies are better made in person. I'll wait to see him at school." She was putting off seeing him, not because she didn't want to apologize, but simply because she needed a break, a chance to catch her breath. Things were moving far too fast for her.

"Or we could go see him tomorrow."

"We've spent so much time with him since you found him. I'd like one day to really sort things through. Plus, didn't you mention going over to Sean's house?"

"Yeah."

"So, why don't you do that, and I'll take tomorrow and get myself straightened around, then next week I'll apologize."

"And if I present my very logical list of reasons I should be allowed to try hockey, will you try to make a decision on that, as well? They're having tryouts next weekend."

"Yes. I'll come to a decision."

"Great, I'll get the list." He paused, ran back to her and

hugged her. "I didn't want you to think that was a bribe. That's just 'cause…" He shrugged. "Just 'cause."

He ran to his room, presumably to get the list.

Michelle pasted a smile on her face.

Daniel had been right.

She was going to have make that apology. And she was going to have to figure out how to let someone else into the tight little circle she and Brandon had formed.

Chapter Nine

Sunday was the longest day in Daniel's life. By ten o'clock he was pacing in the house, and called it quits. He headed into downtown Erie, to the house he was working on, and used the set of keys Josh Christopher, the contractor in charge of the project, had given him to let himself in.

Chloe followed him as he set down his tools. He didn't bother taking off his coat because the heat was off for the weekend since no one was supposed to be here.

For an hour he lost himself in some intricate detail work on the banister.

Chloe's barking shook him from his work. He heard the front door open and moments later, Josh came in.

"I was driving by and saw your truck. It's Sunday, McLean. I don't expect anyone to work on Sunday. Saturday, yes, but never on Sunday. A man should have one day a week when his family can rely on him being around." He must have realized his mistake. "Sorry, Dan, I forgot—"

"It's okay." He thought about telling Josh about Brandon, but sharing wasn't generally something he was good at, even though Josh was friend enough to listen.

Josh pulled up a stepladder and sat on it, peering at Daniel through the banister. "Dating anyone? You must be. The only thing that could cause a guy to look as confused as you do is a woman."

How to explain his relationship with Michelle? "I'm sort of seeing someone. Maybe."

He laughed. "That doesn't sound very definite."

"It's not. Well, it is. I mean, I've been with her every day, pretty much every hour that I wasn't working or sleeping. It's complicated."

"Hey, how complicated could it be? You like her?"

"I do." He set down his chisel with far more force than required.

"She obviously likes you if she's letting you hang around that much. So, if you're dating some new woman and spending every minute you can with her, why on earth are you here on a Sunday and not somewhere with her?"

"We had a falling-out."

"Women." Josh managed to make the word sound like a swearword. "Can't live with them. Can't spend too much time with them without a fight. What was it? Did you forget an anniversary? Not call?"

"I interfered with her nephew." Daniel purposefully didn't mention her nephew could be his son. As soon as he got the test result, he planned to shout it from the rooftops, but not until then. "She's raising him, and had said no to something, and I suggested that maybe she was saying no because it was easier on her, not better for him."

Josh grimaced. "Damn, Daniel, if you're going to screw up, you do it right. I've got to guess she didn't take that well."

"That's an understatement," Daniel agreed morosely.

"So what are you going to do?" Josh asked.

"She said she needed time off. I'll see her Tuesday."

"Well, that's not so bad, then."

"It's not so good."

"Hey, from where I'm sitting, I'm getting an extra day's work from you, so at least one of us is happy." He laughed, then stopped when he saw Daniel hadn't joined in. "You've got it bad."

"It's…well, it's complicated."

"I'm sure it is. When women are involved, it's always complicated. And as the relationship guru…" Josh must have recognized Daniel's skeptical look because he grinned. "Hey, I'm just stating the facts. And as a relationship guru I have some very sage advice. Flowers."

"What?" Daniel asked.

"When you see her, take flowers. And I wouldn't wait until Tuesday."

"That's your advice?"

"Yes. If you don't follow it, then it's on your own head. Flowers always work. Give them to her, and apologize. Even if it wasn't your fault. Almost any relationship issue can be cleared up with flowers and a good apology. Even if I'm not the one who was wrong, I find apologizing advantageous."

Daniel simply nodded. He wasn't sure he'd be willing to apologize just to keep the peace. But in this case, he'd been wrong. Michelle had been very generous, letting him spend time with Brandon.

If he was Brandon's father, he'd want some say, but right now, he was, for all intents and purposes, a stranger. He had no rights. She might have overreacted, but he couldn't blame her. He was an unknown coming into her life and sending it into turmoil.

And Michelle wasn't someone who liked turmoil. Not at all.

The thought made him smile.

"You're thinking about her," Josh said.

Daniel had forgotten that Josh was even there. "Why do you say that?"

"That look. Man, you're totally head over heels for her."

"I'm not," he denied. But the words felt like a lie. He liked her. Liked her a lot. He'd kissed her, even. But head over heels?

Maybe, just maybe he was.

"Man, you should see your face. Just figuring out, huh?" Josh stood. "Well, then my work here is done. Think about it, though. I can see how you feel, so you don't need to tell me. Maybe you should think about telling her."

He walked out of the room, saying, "Flowers, Daniel. Women like that kind of thing."

Daniel didn't think she'd like him taking flowers to her at the school. But tomorrow, there was no school. If he dropped them off at her house, she'd get them in private, and maybe things would be back to normal on Tuesday.

Having some sort of plan was a relief.

Tomorrow, he'd drop flowers off at her house.

MICHELLE HUNG UP the phone and tried to work up some sort of enthusiasm for some quality alone time. It happened so rarely.

She'd taken the day off to spend time with Brandon, but not only had he spent last night over at Sean's, he'd called this morning and asked to go skating with Sean and then dinner with Sean, as well. "Seriously, Michelle, I've got a ton of stuff to do around here," Carly had said. "And having Sean out of my hair with Brandon will make life that much easier. Rhiana's at a friend's and the afternoon will be all mine. I'll drop Brandon off after supper."

What could she say to that? Carly had practically made it seem as if Brandon hanging out with Sean was a favor. "Great. That's great."

"You okay?" Carly asked.

"Sure, I'm fine."

"You don't sound so sure."

Michelle could almost picture Carly frowning on the other end of the line. She hastened to reassure her. "I'm running through a list of things on my when-I've-got-time list of things to do, trying to decide which one to tackle today."

"You could use the time to relax."

"I relax better when I'm doing things." Michelle hesitated. "Oh, I know, I can wrap Brandon's presents. They're at the neighbor's now. I can get them, wrap them and have them hidden before he ever gets back. And to make you happy, I'll order Chinese tonight from Fortune Garden. That work?"

"Very well. And we're still on for Wednesday night?"

"Carly, I wouldn't miss your graduation for anything." Her friend had worked so hard, managing her kids, her job and school. "I'll be there."

"Great. Then we'll see you after dinner when I drop Brandon off."

"See you then." Michelle called the neighbor's and ran over to get Brandon's presents. She pulled out her plastic crate of wrapping supplies and went to it.

The new Wii he'd been begging for since it had come out was the big item. She couldn't wait until he opened it. But he was sly and she didn't want him shaking packages and guessing what it was early. She'd saved boxes for the past few weeks and decided to really make him work for the gift.

She started with a box for a shirt. She put the Wii, wrapped in bubble wrap, in it, and then wrapped it.

Next, she had a box that was slightly bigger that she'd asked for when she'd bought Brandon's new winter coat. She put the wrapped box in it, used newspaper as padding, and wrapped it. She had three more boxes, until she came to the big box her neighbor's new thirty-two-inch flat-screen television had come in. She'd had him save it for her. It was too big to wrap, so instead, she put her package in it, padded it with two bags of recyclable paper, and then duct taped the whole box. She used an entire roll of duct tape. A pretty green duct tape instead of the normal slate-gray. She topped it off with a red bow.

That was definitely festive and it was going to take Brandon forever to get to the Wii inside.

She was just getting ready to lug it to her room, where she'd leave it for Brandon to snoop and find, when the doorbell rang.

She was chuckling to herself, imagining his annoyance at not being able to unwrap it and peek, when she opened the door and saw who it was. "Oh. I thought we weren't getting together until tomorrow." It was a rude greeting and she instantly felt sorry. "Come on in. I was going to call you anyway."

Daniel still hadn't said a word as he handed her a bag that had been sitting at his feet. "Why don't you open this before you tell me why you were going to call."

She motioned him inside, and he entered and shut the door behind him, but didn't make any move to leave the foyer.

Michelle opened the bag and found a giant poinsettia inside. "Daniel, you shouldn't have."

"A friend said that after you annoy a woman, flowers are the best way to say you are sorry."

Well, the fact he'd known she'd been angry—even if he'd called it annoyed—was no surprise. She'd so totally over-reacted. "Now I feel worse."

"You're supposed to feel better because I do apologize."

"You're being nice. And you really don't need to apologize. I was planning to apologize to you." She took a deep breath. "Daniel, you didn't try to tell me what to do, you only offered an opinion. And I overreacted. I'm sorry."

"Forgiven. I should have stepped back and let you handle it. It wasn't my place to say anything."

"No, you were right," she told him, still hugging the poinsettia to her chest. "It's been Brandon and me on our own for so long. When he was little, I made unilateral decisions about what was best for him. Somewhere along the line, he grew up, and I didn't notice. I mean, he's still a child and I still have the ultimate say-so, but he's old enough to have some say. I have to learn to listen better. You made me do that, listen to what mattered to him."

"And what did you decide?" Daniel asked.

"That I'd let him try out. And because I'm such a bad aunt, I'm going to be saying my prayers that he sucks."

Daniel chuckled. "Yeah, that sounds like a plan."

"Do you want to come in? All the way in?"

"I didn't mean to intrude. I know we've been spending quite a lot of time together recently and I don't blame you for needing some space. Ours has been a whirlwind…" He let the sentence die off, as if he didn't know how to define exactly what they were.

"Please, come in. You're right, we have been in each other's company, but rarely alone. Brandon is at Sean's. That's Carly's son. He won't be home until after dinner, and I've been rattling around the house. If you come in, we'll have some time to talk."

She thought he was going to leave, but the moment passed, and he nodded.

"Great. Do you want something to drink?" she asked.

"I'm fine." He took off his boots and coat. He hesitated before putting the coat on the hook.

"Problem?"

"I thought the other night that this was the hook I hung my coat up on every time I came here. It's starting to feel…normal? Familiar. As if I'd claimed it for my own."

She knew what he meant. They'd fit in together quickly. It felt almost surreal.

"Daniel, I hereby bequeath you that hook. It's yours to use any time you come over." She tried to make a joke, but it fell flat.

Daniel laughed anyway. "Thanks. You've been very gracious about this entire situation. I'd hoped we'd have some news today, but there was nothing in the mail."

"Here, either." Before she lost her nerve, she said, "About the other night. Thanks. Brandon and I talked, really talked, when we got home. He said he needed to see if hockey was what he was meant to do. That he wanted what you and I had found. You and your woodworking and me…"

"What did he say you were meant to do?"

She melted all over again, remembering. "He said that raising him was what I was meant to do."

She turned and walked into the living room, leaving Daniel to follow her, giving herself time to compose herself. She sat on the couch, and he sat on the other end. "I hope what I was meant to do, more than carpentry, is being a father to Brandon. If the test says I am, what then?"

"I don't know. I mean, at first I was so afraid because I didn't know you. I didn't know what kind of man you were. Now I do. And as much as that's a comfort, I still don't know how we're going to make this work."

"And if the test comes back and I'm not Brandon's father? Are you going to kick me to the curb?"

"What?" The question wasn't one she'd expected.

"You don't know what to do with me if I am Brandon's father, so what if I'm not? Do you have a more definite idea what you're going to do with me then?"

"I don't understand. What do you want me to say?"

"Listen, I opened the door and found Brandon on the porch asking if I was his father. I had no idea what I was getting myself into, but I knew that if I was his father, I'd take responsibility. I know what it's like to have a father who doesn't care. Who just walks away. I couldn't do that to my kid. Now, I'm pretty sure I can't walk away no matter what that test shows. You two have come to mean something to me."

She wanted to ask what but couldn't find the words.

Daniel leaned across the couch and gently touched her cheek with his work-roughed hand. "And it's not only Brandon, though I really do care for him. It's you, too, Michelle. You all on your own, apart from him. You mean something to me." He trailed his finger down her cheek. "We've skirted around this attraction. As if we could ignore it. But, Michelle, I can't ignore it anymore."

She placed her hand on top of his and gently pulled it from her cheek. She pulled it below her shoulder level, when he stopped cooperating and moved his hand, and the other, around the back of her neck. Then gently, not forcing the issue, he pulled her to him. Slowly, with the lightest of touches. Leaving her all the time in the world to move away. To stop this from going where she sensed it might be going.

The problem was, she didn't want to stop it.

Brandon was right, she'd been programmed to be the good sister. To follow the rules and never make impetuous decisions.

This one time, she didn't want to analyze, didn't want a list…she just wanted to jump. She knew if she did, Daniel would catch her.

She moved forward and, when their lips met, the touch was what she'd somehow known it would be. A perfect fit.

This time, the kiss began as softly as the first one, but soon became intimate. Desire was there. Attraction. And not just a physical attraction. Everything about Daniel McLean touched her. And touching him like this, running her fingers along the curve of his back as he bent slightly to kiss her, felt right.

It felt good.

It felt like coming home.

She'd heard that phrase before. And she knew what it meant. She felt that way every time she pulled into her driveway. It wasn't the house that was her home. It was knowing Brandon was there. He was home.

And this man, this practical stranger, felt the same way.

Daniel pulled back from the kiss and it felt like a physical loss. "I want you," he said, his voice husky with need. "I know we haven't known each other long. And I'm willing to wait if that's what you want. But if that is what you want, pulling back from this—from you—will be the hardest thing I've ever done."

The rational side of Michelle knew she should say, *No, we can't.* She should pull back, walk away. And up until now, she'd always felt that her rational side made up the greatest percentage of who she was. Although right now, she wasn't thinking with logic as she said, "Yes. I don't want to talk this to death. I don't want to analyze. I just want you."

She stood and, feeling totally out of character, she took his hand and led him to her room. She thought about saying something, but she couldn't think of anything to say. Obviously, neither could he. They were silent as they entered the bedroom.

Michelle stood there awkwardly for a moment, then he took her other hand in his and pulled her against him.

That's all it took.

They kissed again. A long introduction to what was to come.

Michelle leaned down and threw the throw pillows on the bed onto the floor, for the first time wishing she hadn't made the bed, because unmaking it took too long. Finally, they sank in unison to her bed and then slowly, as they kissed, they took their clothes off, never totally releasing each other as they did, as if they both feared that breaking their connection would spoil the moment.

"Are you sure we're not making a mistake?" she asked, needing to hear him say they weren't. Needing his confidence in what they were doing to bolster her own.

"Hell no, but I'm not going to stop…unless you want to?"

"Hell no," she echoed. And though it wasn't an overly funny statement on either of their parts, they both laughed. A quiet chuckle at first, then finally full-blown belly laughs.

Michelle had never laughed while making love. She'd never even considered that laughter was missing from other relationships. But now, here in Daniel's arms as she laughed, their lovemaking became something more than she'd ever experienced. Something fun and tender.

It touched her in a way she couldn't quite decipher and analyze. And as she relaxed in Daniel's arms, she didn't even try. For once, she simply allowed herself to accept the here and now.

And here and now, she was totally content.

DANIEL STARED at the incredible woman in his arms. She'd fallen asleep after they'd made love for the second time.

She was the most open, giving woman. Not that it surprised him. Michelle gave of herself continuously—with Brandon, at school, with her friends.

When he looked back on this first time with Michelle he knew he'd remember her laughter. And the way she'd looked up at him. Everything was there in that one look. He could read her better than he ever had.

She'd wanted this. She was afraid of what it would mean, but she hadn't let that stop her.

And there was something else there, as well.

Something he hoped he was reading right. She cared for him.

At that moment he realized just how much she'd come to mean to him.

He admired her. She was a strong, independent woman, able to stand on her own two feet and yet able to open her heart to a nephew she hadn't even known existed.

She was beautiful. Not in a loud, fashion-model beauty. No, hers was a quieter type. The kind that required you to see beyond the businesslike facade she wore so easily.

He cared about her. Cared about her in a way that didn't involve Brandon—whether or not he was Brandon's father.

Caring didn't seem a strong enough word.

He was considering other definitions of his feeling for Michelle, when her eyes sprang open.

It was like a blind that had sprung back up.

Gone was the relaxed, confident, laughing woman he'd just made love to. In her place was a woman who looked at the clock with panic in her expression. "Brandon's supposed to be home in ten minutes."

"What?"

"Ten minutes. Carly's bringing him home." She paused a moment, then added, "And we're naked, Daniel." She was already sitting up, ready to jump into action.

"Deep breath, Michelle. I'm sure we can de-naked ourselves in ten minutes," he joked.

But the joke fell flat. She *was* in a panic. "Come on, move!" She was already scooping up clothes and hurrying into the bathroom.

He got out of bed and even went so far as to remake Michelle's bed. It didn't look quite the same as when they'd come in. He suspected he'd done the myriad pillows wrong, but it was close.

"Hurry up, downstairs," she called.

He followed her back down the stairs and into the living room. As they entered he noticed she'd been wrapping gifts. There was a pile of department-store bags, as well as a couple wrapped presents. "How about I help you wrap? It will look totally innocent when Brandon comes in."

She nodded and hurried to the pile. "Here." She thrust a bookstore bag at him. "Wrap this one."

He opened the bag and found a beautiful edition of Herbert's *Dune.* "Oh, I loved this book."

Michelle was busily opening another bag but looked up. "Oh, yes. Me, too. Brandon's started reading a lot of science fiction lately. I thought this was a good choice."

He wanted her to relax, so he tried to distract her from her anxiety by asking, "Did you get him the rest of the series?"

"I thought I'd let him try this one out, and if he liked it, I'd buy more."

"Oh." Daniel had been wondering about gifts the past few days. "What's in the big one?"

"A gaming system he wanted." She glanced at the gift and smiled, finally seeming as if she'd calmed down. "It's wrapped in a bunch of boxes, and there's duct tape involved. I didn't want him guessing."

"It wasn't simply that you didn't want him to guess what it was—you enjoy driving him nuts, too."

"Guilty as charged. An added benefit. Brandon is very adept at unwrapping and rewrapping gifts to peek. I enjoy making it tough."

"I've been trying to decide what to give him."

"Daniel, I know this sounds totally syrupy, but really, the

biggest gift you could give him, you already have. A gift of time, and concern. That's the best."

"Thanks." He paused, not wanting to throw her back into a state of panic but needing to know. "Michelle, about what just happened."

"Sorry. I… From the little things Brandon has said, Tara wasn't overly discreet with her boyfriends. He was still little, but I'm sure it was confusing. I had a boyfriend when he came to live with me, but he didn't stick around. He didn't want to be tied down with a kid, so we broke up. There have been dates since, but nothing like…" She hesitated. "Nothing serious. Brandon's older now, but I still wouldn't want to do anything to confuse him. And now that we've got that out of our system, we won't need to worry about it happening again."

"Out of our system?" Daniel was about to inform her that making love to her didn't purge the fact that he wanted her. It intensified it. "Michelle—"

"Oh, there's lights in the driveway. That's got to be them. Can you finish off the present before he comes in? I don't want him to see." And with that she practically bounded to the door.

Saved by the headlights, he thought as he wrapped the book.

Not really saved. She'd simply forestalled the conversation that he was going to have with her.

He heard her open the door and heard Brandon say, "Where's Dan?"

"He's in the living room wrapping one of your gifts, so don't go charging in until he tells you it's clear."

There was a thud and some noise, and Daniel hurriedly got the book covered in paper.

"Hey, Dan, I'm home. Aunt Shell said to be sure it's clear before I come in."

"Give me a second to tape this last side." He folded the edge into a little triangle, and pulled it to the back of the book, then taped it down. "All clear. You won't know what it is."

Brandon ran into the room. "Hey, I didn't think you were coming over today, or else I'd've come straight home."

"I haven't been here that long."

"There's a lot of snow on your car."

He felt stuck for an answer. "Well, I guess I've been here long enough to get snow on the car, but I was helping with Christmas wrapping, so the time passed fast."

"Hey, what's this one?" He pointed to the package Michelle had said contained his gaming system.

Michelle grinned. "Daniel's been sworn to secrecy, so no grilling him for hints."

"Maybe a little hint?" Brandon wheedled.

"Sure," Michelle said, a teasing glint in her eye. "Whatever's in that box is smaller than a car."

"I bet Dan can come up with a better hint than that," he groused.

"Sure," Daniel said, getting into the rhythm of Michelle's idea of a hint. "Whatever's in that package is bigger than a nail."

"Come on you, two."

Michelle smiled a wicked grin. "It's smaller than a whale and it's not alive."

"It's bigger than a pebble," Daniel added helpfully, "but not as round."

"Yeah, you two are soooo funny," Brandon said in a way that let them know they weren't funny at all to him. "I'm glad you're enjoying this."

"Adults learn early on to take their pleasures wherever they can." At the word *pleasure* Michelle glanced at him, then turned a lovely shade of pink.

The fact she was blushing was sweet. It touched something in Daniel.

"I'm going to put my stuff away if you need to finish up in here," Brandon said.

"Give me five minutes…no cheating and trying to peek," Michelle warned.

"As if. I'm not a kid anymore, Aunt Shell." He stomped toward the hallway.

"Oh, I forgot. You're so old now," she called after him.

Brandon turned around. "Hey, I'll be driving in three years."

The smirk disappeared from Michelle's face. "That was just mean, Bran."

"She hates me talking about that," Brandon said to Daniel. "She doesn't want to teach me."

"It's not so much I don't want to teach you as it is I'm terrified of teaching you."

Daniel found himself offering, "I could help with that, if you like."

The implication that he'd still be around three years from now wasn't lost on Michelle. He could see it in her expression. "We have a lot of time before we have to worry about driving lessons," she said. "Right now, go put your stuff away, Bran, while I clean up in here."

Brandon ran out of the room and up the stairs.

"Michelle, I noticed."

"Noticed what?" She took the couple presents yet unwrapped and stuffed them in a bag, then took the bag to the coffee table, which was very chestlike. She opened it, shuffled around some blankets and stuffed the remaining gifts underneath.

He waited until she finished. "Michelle." She finally looked at him. "I'm not going anywhere. I'm not waiting for some test result to decide. I'm in this, unless you kick me out." He wanted to add, *Don't kick me out,* but it sounded rather pathetic even as he thought it, so he refrained.

"It's easy to say you're in now. It's only been a couple weeks. There's a sense of novelty to having a boy who thinks you hung the moon. But how about a month from now? Six months? What if you're busy at work, or busy with a new relationship? What if Brandon's going through a rebellious phase and driving you nuts? Don't make promises you might have to break."

"Michelle." He stood and walked over to her and gently took her face in his hand. "I need you to pay attention here. I'm not the kind of guy who walks away. Tara left me and never told me about Brandon, or I'd have been here all along. I know you get busy during tax season, right? That doesn't mean you shuffle Brandon off on someone else. You make it work. Well, I'm planning to make it work, whether he's mad at me, or I'm busy. I'm in it. As for the comment about a new relationship, I'm not looking for one of those."

"Sometimes you're not looking and they just fall into your lap." She broke the contact, bending to finish cleaning up the paper.

"I know," Daniel said softly. "I wasn't looking for one when I found—"

"All clear?" Brandon called from the steps.

When I found you—that's how he'd planned to finish the sentence. But since Brandon was right outside the room, he didn't. "We'll finish this discussion later."

Chapter Ten

Daniel hadn't been sure what sort of reception he'd get on Tuesday. He kind of hoped Michelle would go all soft and doe-eyed when he walked in. Maybe she'd blush again. Instead, she was in her professional mode.

She was polite.

Nice even.

She spoke to him. No, she spoke *at* him. She didn't talk *to* him. It was as if she had a bubble around her. He could see her through it, but he couldn't get close.

"Can we do dinner tonight?" he asked over the hot glue gun he was using to affix tiny red bows to the punched-tin ornaments. She glanced at Brandon, who'd obviously overheard his quiet question and was nodding so hard Daniel wondered if his neck would be injured.

"Sure," she said.

After they finished their craft-a-thon, they headed back to the Cornerstone. Brandon had kept the conversation going, talking excitedly about hockey tryouts.

"I have a favor to ask," Michelle said when Brandon went to the restroom.

"Anything."

"Tomorrow, Carly graduates in the evening. I wondered if you might like to watch Brandon? He's too old for a babysitter, but Carly, Samantha and I were going to go out afterward, and I hate leaving him alone all night."

"That's not you asking me for a favor, that's you doing me one. Thanks. I'd love to. The two of us can manage dinner and homework."

"You're sure it won't be an inconvenience?" she asked, as if she hoped he'd say yes.

"Are you sure you want me to?" he countered.

"Of course, I do, or I wouldn't have asked."

"Then, yes. I'll be there after school, and if you don't mind, I'll take Brandon back to my place for dinner, and then we'll come into town and I'll just hang out and wait for you to come home."

"His bedtime is ten, although we don't call it a bedtime," she warned with the ghost of a smile. "Thirteen is too old for bedtimes."

"I'll see to it."

"Thanks."

"No, thank you." He knew he should just leave well enough alone, but he added, "Can we talk…I mean really talk, about yesterday?"

"We should," she said reluctantly. Her expression said she'd rather do just about anything else. "I—"

"Hey, are we doing dessert?" Brandon asked as he returned from the restroom.

The moment was broken, but Daniel promised himself they'd talk soon. Tomorrow night after she got back from her friend's graduation, they'd have their talk, whether she liked it or not.

"OH, COME ON." Carly shook her head as she drove the minivan and glanced into the back seat. "Seriously, Samantha, turn off the waterworks."

"But you just graduated," Samantha blubbered from the back seat, sitting between Sean and Rhiana. "You, Carly Lewis, are a nurse. You're a sister nurse." She leaned forward and hugged Carly around the seat, not for the first time.

"If we get in an accident, I'm going to be an R.N. who never gets to practice," Carly grumbled, though Michelle was pretty sure, she was enjoying the fuss, even though she'd never admit it.

Michelle was sitting in the front passenger seat, and was less huggy but just as emotional. She wouldn't have thought she would be, but watching Carly walk across the stage and move her tassel from one side to the other touched her. She could imagine Brandon doing the same thing in four years, graduating from high school. Then again, four years after that when he graduated from college, too.

"Tonight, we're celebrating," Carly announced. "A raucous celebration, not a maudlin one."

"Okay, Webster," Rhiana said with the perfect teen I'm-embarrassed-by-my-mother inflection. "We know you're a college graduate, you don't have to pull out all your five-dollar words to remind us."

"Tonight I will definitely be using every five-dollar word in my repertoire," Carly assured her with undisguised glee. "I am Samantha's sister nurse. A nicely signed diploma that I plan to take to North American Gallery next week and get framed as my Christmas present to myself."

"Don't listen to her, Mom," Sean said. "We're proud of you."

"Suck-up," Rhiana groused.

"Kids, we have guests in the car, and only a few more minutes until we get to your father's house. Do you think you can behave that long and impress Mrs. Williams and Ms. Hamilton with how sweet my children are?"

"It'll be tough, Mom, but I'll try," Sean teased. "I'm sure they've already noticed my sweetness. I mean, come on, Mom, how could they miss it?"

"Stuck up, suck-up," Rhiana repeated.

"Sorry, Samantha and Michelle. My children have no manners."

"But we do have a mother who's a nurse, so maybe we'll learn to be compassionate?" Rhiana teased. "Compassion is better than manners."

"Both attributes are preferable," Carly said with prim teasing.

"Webster," Rhiana muttered loud enough to be sure her mother heard her.

Five minutes later, the kids were dropped off at Carly's ex's, and the three of them went to Colao's for a late dinner.

"Wear your cap," Samantha told Carly as they got out in front of the westside restaurant. "You don't have to wear the gown, but come on, give me a thrill…wear the cap."

"You two are crazy." Carly reached back into the van and retrieved her cap.

"Yeah, but wear it anyway," Samantha told her.

"And use your five-dollar words," Michelle teased. "They make you sound very collegiate."

"Fine. You two are severely sanity challenged. Unbalanced. Unhinged. Demented."

"Hey, don't forget good old insane," Samantha called out helpfully as they went into the restaurant. She looked at the hostess and said very loudly, "We'd like your best table for my friend, the college graduate."

"Oh, hey, that's great! Mercyhurst, right? I heard the college was having its graduation tonight. I thought a Wednesday night was odd."

"The Warner's got some renovations going on, so we had it at the new Bayfront Convention Center, but they were booked for the weekends, hence a Wednesday night," Carly said. "Probably more than you needed to know."

"Hey, I asked. What's your degree in?" The hostess led them to a booth.

"She's a nurse," Samantha piped in.

"Not until I pass my state boards."

"Close enough," Samantha assured both Carly and the hostess.

"What's her name?" the hostess asked Michelle in a hushed tone.

"Carly." Michelle crawled into the booth and set Carly's diploma up against the wall. "Look at that. It's a thing of beauty."

"Hey, everyone," the hostess called loudly. "I'd like a big hand for my friend Carly here. She just graduated from Mercyhurst with her nursing degree."

Carly hung her head. "I'm so embarrassed."

"You'll survive," Michelle told her. "We're so proud of you."

"Hmm, you know what Dean said when I dropped off the kids?"

"No, what did the rat bastard say?" Samantha had a snarl to her voice that would have sounded more at home in Carly's. They both had a grudge against Dean for the way he'd treated Carly.

"He said congratulations, and added he was so happy I graduated. He waited a moment and said that he was glad because he'd written my last tuition check and I was officially done sponging off him."

Michelle knew that Carly had quit college the first time to put Dean through law school and, according to their divorce settlement, he was responsible for paying for her tuition now.

"What a lovely guy," Michelle muttered.

"Speaking of lovely guys, how's Daniel?" Carly asked with a wicked grin.

"That's the question I've been really waiting for you to ask, even while I've been dreading it," Michelle admitted. "I've made a real mess of it where he's concerned."

And she let it all spill out. Her worries, her over-the-top reaction to Daniel's hockey intervention. "I felt like the smallest person on the planet. Rather than be happy that this man who might very well be Brandon's father is a fantastic, honorable guy, I felt threatened."

"It's a complicated situation," Samantha told her.

"I think I made it more complicated. You see we—"

"You kissed him. You kissed him good and proper," Carly guessed. "You kissed his socks off."

"More than that," Michelle admitted morosely.

"More than his socks?" Carly asked, as the realization sank in. "Oh."

"Oh," Samantha echoed.

"Oh," Michelle assured them. "I don't know how it happened."

"I assumed someone had explained the birds and the bees to you before this," Carly said, "but here goes. When a man likes a woman, and she likes him—"

"Carly," Samantha said sternly, "can't you see you're not helping?"

"Sorry." Carly didn't quite sound as if she was truly sorry. "I mean, I can see you're upset, but really, Michelle, he's gorgeous. You both are single. Tell us more."

"I don't kiss and tell," Michelle said primly.

"Party pooper. Tonight's my night, and I should be indulged at every turn."

"Please forgive our ebullient friend," Samantha said on Carly's behalf. "See, I have a few five-dollar words, too. Now, Michelle, tell us whatever you're comfortable sharing."

"Suffice it to say, it was a huge mistake." The rational part of her knew that taking her relationship with Daniel to a physical level added one more level of complexity to their already overly complex relationship. Although a totally foreign, seldom-glimpsed side of her couldn't help but remember the sweetness of being with Daniel.

"Huge mistakes are generally the best kind," Carly teased.

Samantha ignored Carly and simply asked, "Why, Michelle?"

"Think about the situation we're in. Daniel and I have been thrown together. We still haven't received the test result, so there's no way of knowing if he is or isn't Brandon's father. If he is, and we start anything, then it doesn't work out? Things could be awkward or, worse, untenable. If he's not and I'm seeing him, can you imagine how that will hurt Brandon?"

"From everything you've told us, Brandon likes Daniel. No matter what the test result says, it sounds as if Daniel's been good for Brandon," Samantha reminded her.

"I'm not the type of woman who kisses men I barely know…much less more than that. It hasn't even been quite a month and we…well, we definitely did more than that. That's not me."

"I don't know that time matters when it comes to attraction," Carly said.

"Attraction or more," Samantha added.

"There's no more. Maybe some attraction, but no more," Michelle hastily assured them.

"Look at Harry and me. I met him when school started. Three months is all, and here we are. I can't imagine my life without him. Time doesn't seem important when you find the one—"

"Wait, wait," Michelle said with a sense of panic. "I never said Daniel was the one."

"You've been with him practically every day for weeks."

"I didn't see him Sunday."

Samantha ignored her. "You're together right after work, eat meals together. He's even watching Brandon tonight. It might not have been much time, but some people date for months and don't spend as much time together."

Daniel had made that same point, but Michelle wasn't buying it. "I thought we were here to celebrate Carly's degree, not analyze my relationship with Daniel."

"We're moms," Carly said. "We know how to multitask."

There was no fighting it. Her friends were going to help, whether she wanted them to or not. And the truth was, she did want their opinions. But she wanted their opinions to be she should maintain her distance. She wanted their opinions to be the last man on earth she should be kissing was Daniel McLean.

That's what she wanted.

"Listen, it's been a long time since I was in a serious relationship. I don't know if I'm ready for another one. I have work, and Brandon. There's not much time left over."

"And yet, you and Daniel seem to be managing," Carly said.

"What happened with the last guy?" Samantha asked.

"Brandon happened." It seemed like a thousand years ago. "Max and I wanted to work in some big city. After we graduated, we put out applications, waiting and hoping we'd both get offered jobs in the same big city. And we did. D.C. We were beside ourselves. Then Tara and Brandon showed up on my door. I asked Max to wait. When they didn't need me anymore, I'd come."

"But he didn't wait?" Samantha asked.

"He left without me."

"Men." In that one word, Carly managed to imbue her total

disgust with the whole gender. "Max is your Dean. A caution-ary tale that reminds a woman what happens when you get too invested in a man. They leave you high and dry. Enjoy your time with Daniel McLean, but don't enjoy it so much you lose yourself in him."

Samantha gave Carly a nudge. "Don't listen to her, Michelle. All that showed was that Max wasn't the man for you. Maybe Daniel is. And before you tell me that it's too soon, I'll remind you again that the heart doesn't own a watch. Love is love."

Love is love.

Michelle tried not to groan. She'd never mentioned love. She cared for Daniel. And obviously was attracted to him. But love?

She turned the subject to the Christmas Fair and was thankful both Carly and Samantha were willing to move on to a new topic.

She wasn't prepared for Carly swooning over just how kissable Daniel was but warning her to not fall too deeply, and Samantha repeating that time didn't make much difference when it came to matters of the heart, and throwing her relationship— her very good relationship—with Harry up as an example.

It wasn't what she wanted, but it's what she got. Well, that and a headache.

The evening wound down and Carly drove them both home. They dropped off Samantha first, then Carly drove to Michelle's. "Thanks for the ride."

"Hey, before you get out," Carly said, "I wanted to say something."

"Okay."

"And I don't want you to get mad about it."

"That particular statement never bodes well. It's something Brandon might say."

"Sean and Rhiana have been known to use it, as well. It's just that Samantha's so hot over Harry she practically had you and Daniel walking to an altar. Her relationship with Harry colors her view. It's obvious to both of us, even if she doesn't seem to notice it. Though right now, I'm about the most anti-love person you can find."

"I'm sorry about you and Dean."

Carly shrugged. "I'll get over him, eventually. But the fact that I'm so not a fan of the male race means my opinion is tainted in the opposite direction. You have a lot of great excuses to keep your distance from Daniel. And I agree with them, for what it's worth—well, sort of."

"Just sort of?"

"If we were talking about you hypothetically, or talking about me, I'd agree a hundred percent. But I've seen the two of you together. And, Michelle, despite my current antiman stance, I find I have to side with Samantha. Don't let issues of time, or even of Brandon's parentage, scare you away from something that could be great…something we all see when we look at you and Daniel together."

"I'm not—"

"And don't let fear of being hurt stop you, either. Now, out of the car. This has gotten far too emotional for me, and this college graduate has to get home. Thanks for a great evening."

Michelle didn't know what to make of Carly's statements. "Thanks for including me…and for the advice."

"Well, you should take that advice because I am a college graduate. That means my opinions are now weighted with all that very expensive wisdom."

Michelle laughed as she shut the door. She stood in the driveway as Carly backed out onto the street and drove out of sight.

It was snowing again. She looked up and the snowflakes

twinkled in the streetlight. When she was younger, she'd loved watching the snow. She'd simply enjoyed the beauty of it. Then, she'd gotten older and the beauty had taken a back seat to the shoveling, and the difficult driving the snow caused. She let the cons outweigh the beauty. Was she doing that with Daniel? Letting the what-ifs outweigh the what-might-be?

"Are you coming in?"

Daniel stood at the front door, staring at her.

She hadn't heard him there. "Sorry. I was lost in thought."

"Why don't you come think in here where it's warm?"

She did and, before she could take off her coat and boots, Chloe let her know she expected to be greeted first. Michelle knelt down and petted the dog.

"She missed you. She knew you were supposed to be here, and felt your absence. She was sleeping with Brandon, and hurried down when she heard the car in the driveway."

Michelle buried her face in the dog's thick winter coat. "Thanks, Chloe."

"She wasn't the only one who missed you tonight."

She looked up at Daniel. His expression was so sincere. She didn't know what to say to that.

What was it about Daniel McLean that regularly left her feeling tongue-tied? "Thanks for staying with Brandon. Like I said, I know he's too old for a sitter and I rarely go out, so it's not a big issue. But when I'm gone this long…well, with you here, I didn't have to worry."

She stood and Chloe, sensing her petting was over, walked back up the stairs. Michelle went ahead and took off her coat and boots.

"How was Carly's graduation?" Daniel asked as they walked into the living room.

"Great. Her kids were there, and we took them to their dad's afterward, and then the three of us went for a late dinner at Colao's. Their food's wonderful. And we made Carly wear her cap in and, much to her chagrin and our delight, the hostess announced her graduation to the entire restaurant."

"Sounds like fun." Daniel sat down on the middle cushion of the couch.

Michelle either had to sit on one of the end cushions—right next to Daniel—or sit in a chair and appear afraid to sit next to Daniel. She reluctantly opted for the couch. "How did your night with Brandon go?"

"He borrowed his friend's Wii and taught me to play golf. And I'm supposed to tell you what an excellent gaming system it is because you actually get up and move in order to play it, so you get exercise." He laughed. "I think that's supposed to be a hint. An oh-so-subtle one."

She nodded. "You're going to feel that golf game tomorrow. It's a whole different set of muscles."

She ignored the fact that Daniel's thigh was just inches from hers and was starting to relax, when he said, "Talking about Brandon is always welcome, but is there any chance we're going to talk about this thing between us?"

"I'd really rather not. And I'd rather not admit to the fact that I was a shrew this weekend about your giving an opinion about Brandon, but I was, so I'll apologize for that."

"You weren't a shrew, but you're right, we're going to have to figure out where I fit in, what kind of say I get to have…if any," he hastily added. "But I'd really like to talk about the attraction between us, about when we—"

She could deny there was an attraction, but it would be a lie, and she was sure he'd know that. So rather than trying to deny it, she shook her head. "It's almost eleven, and I have to get up for work tomorrow."

"We're going to have to talk about it eventually, Michelle."

"Yes, we do, but not tonight."

"Fine. Not tonight." He looked disappointed but didn't argue. He got up and went back to the entryway and retrieved his coat from the hook. He put it on and had his hand on the door, when he turned around and kissed her. Just pulled her into his arms and kissed her.

Michelle knew in some faraway rational part of her brain that she should pull back and end the kiss. She was so confused and conflicted, this wasn't helping. But she didn't end it. As a matter of fact, she put her arms around his neck and deepened the kiss. Wanting nothing more than to be standing here in Daniel's arms.

Finally, Daniel was the one to break the kiss. "I'd say we can skip the talk and simply acknowledge that there is indeed attraction between the two of us. All that leaves for us to talk about is how do we handle it."

Before she could say anything, he turned around and opened the door. "Come on, Chloe," he called up the stairs.

There was no response. Daniel turned to Michelle. "Want me to go get her?"

"No, she can spend the night. I can—"

"I'll pick her up in the morning." And without another word about their kiss, he turned and left.

Michelle shut the door, but rather than going upstairs, she stood at the window and watched as his truck pulled out of her driveway and disappeared down the street.

Just weeks ago, her life was orderly and had a rhythm that she knew and understood. Now, Brandon had a potential father, there was a dog sleeping in his room and she'd been thoroughly kissed by a man she knew she should be keeping away from.

How on earth had that happened?

How was she going to get her life back on track?

And the biggest question of all…did she really want to go back to the way things were?

Chapter Eleven

Daniel was at Michelle's front door at seven the next morning. "Brandon said you don't leave to take him to school until seven thirty-five." He didn't mention that when Brandon gave him such a specific time, he was sure it was because Michelle left precisely at seven thirty-five, not seven thirty-six or -seven. Not even a few minutes early.

He found the thought cute.

But as she frowned at him, he very wisely chose not to share the fact that her punctuality and preciseness delighted him.

"I brought doughnuts," he said, holding the box aloft. "I thought I'd trade the doughnuts for a cup of coffee before Chloe and I go to work."

She looked surprised, but then said, "Uh, okay."

As Daniel took his coat off, Brandon came barreling down the stairs with Chloe on his heels. "Hey, Dan. I got up early and took Chloe out for a walk. Aunt Shell said she didn't want to leave me last night."

"No, she didn't, the traitor." He leaned down and petted Chloe. "But hey, it gave me an excuse to drop by with dough-nuts. Mighty Fine Donuts. I got a selection because I didn't know which ones you liked."

"I like 'em all," Brandon assured him with a grin. "But the creamed-filled are my favorites."

"I'm sure there's some of those."

Brandon took the box and sprinted toward the kitchen. "Thanks," he called over his shoulder.

Chloe appeared unsure for a moment, looking up at Daniel, then after Brandon, before she took off after the boy.

"Fruit first," Michelle hollered.

Daniel was still standing at the entryway, holding his coat. "Are you coming?"

Daniel grinned, kicked off his boots and hung his coat on the hook. His hook.

Brandon was at the counter, staring inside the doughnut box as he chewed a banana. He shoved the last half in his mouth and, as he chewed it, took a cream-filled doughnut from the box.

"These are great, Dan," he said, around the still impressive amount of food in his mouth.

"Wait until you've finished chewing," Michelle scolded as she set a glass of milk in front of him, then a mug of coffee in front of Daniel.

They ate their doughnuts and Brandon complained about his big science test. "Right before Christmas. That's not fair."

"Better before than right after the Christmas break. You'd have to spend your whole holiday studying," Michelle pointed out as she took a sip of coffee.

"I guess you're right." He glanced up at the clock. "Oh, man, we're leaving in ten minutes." He shoved the rest of his doughnut in his mouth and said, "Thanks, Dan."

At least that's what Daniel thought he said.

"Brandon, not with your mouth full," Michelle scolded again.

Daniel laughed. "You can keep saying it, but it doesn't appear to be working."

"I can live in hope that someday it will," she said, having a last sip of coffee, then taking the cup to the sink, rinsing it and putting it in the dishwasher.

She came back for the dishes Brandon had left.

"Listen, Michelle—" He could see her tense up as he said the words. He assumed she thought he was going to talk about their relationship again, but he'd decided not to. Talking just gave her a chance to argue against it. So, no more talking, but hopefully a lot more kissing. "We've got almost everything done for the Christmas Fair, so I thought maybe after school, I could pick up the two of you in my truck and we could get Christmas trees for your place and for mine."

"Daniel, you don't have to—"

He cut her off. "I want to. Unless you don't."

She paused a moment, then admitted, "No, I want to, too."

"Then I'll be here a little after three. Maybe you two could come back to my place and help me set mine up?" He waited, sure she was going to say no.

"Fine."

He leaned forward and kissed her, very carefully keeping it light. "Thanks."

Daniel was going to try to keep things casual and ease Michelle into the idea that he wasn't going anywhere. It didn't matter what the test came back saying. He'd realized that he was in this. He cared for Michelle and Brandon. He didn't need a test to tell him they were supposed to be his family.

He knew it was fast, and he was willing to accept that it might take Michelle a little longer to figure that out.

Brandon ran back into the kitchen, and though they were no longer touching, Michelle took a step back, increasing the distance between them.

"Okay, Aunt Shell, I'm ready." Brandon tossed a book bag onto the stool and glanced at the clock. "Two minutes to spare."

"He likes to try and beat the clock," Michelle told Daniel.

"Your aunt said it would be okay with her if the three of us went to get trees tonight together. Then we'll grab a pizza and the two of you can come help me set mine up."

"And then you're coming here to help us with ours?"

"Why don't we wait until this weekend to set ours up, Bran. After your hockey tryouts?" Michelle was gathering up her things for work. "Setting up one tree in a day is enough."

"Okay. But you'll come help, right, Dan?"

Daniel looked at Michelle and she nodded.

"You couldn't keep me from it."

THE CHRISTMAS TREE shopping had been a success, and Daniel's looked great in his living room. He had ornaments his grandfather had carved, and every year he did a new one himself. He was hoping hockey tryout day went as well.

Saturday morning, Daniel was prompt when he picked them up and drove Brandon to the ice rink for his tryout. Brandon rambled excitedly in the back of the truck as they parked in front of the rink.

Michelle turned around in her seat. "Do you have everything?"

"Yes. You asked me before we left the house, too." Brandon heaved a sigh that said he was too old to be babied.

"Sorry." She unbuckled her seat belt and started to open her door.

"Aunt Shell, you can't come in," Brandon said, horror in his voice. "You've signed the forms and I have them in my bag. I go in alone. You and Dan can go somewhere and just come pick me up in three hours."

"Oh." Her hand slipped from the door handle. "Yes, of course."

"I'll buy you brunch," Daniel offered.

She smiled. "Thanks. That would be nice."

"Good luck," he said to Brandon, then looked at Michelle, knowing that she wasn't exactly hoping Brandon made the team.

"Yes, good luck. We'll be back in three hours then. You don't leave the rink for any reason until we're back."

"The coaches wouldn't let me even if I wanted to," Brandon assured her.

They both watched until Brandon was safely inside the ice arena.

"So, how about that brunch?" Daniel asked, wanting to pin her down because she looked, for all intents and purposes, like someone who was ready to bolt.

"You don't have to do that." Her gaze was still locked on the rink's doors. Either she was afraid Brandon was going to make a break for it, or she wanted to avoid looking at Daniel.

"I want to have brunch with you," he said.

"Fine."

"Ah, Michelle, your enthusiasm is touching," he teased.

She finally looked at him and laughed as he put the car into Drive.

The sound brought to mind making love with her and his body tightened.

He concentrated on driving. That was definitely safer than thinking about making love to Michelle.

He pulled out of the parking lot and turned east onto Thirty-Eighth Street.

"I just figured we'd grab something on Peach Street," she said as she noticed they were heading in the opposite direction.

Peach Street was populated with restaurants, and the ice rink was practically around the corner, so he understood why she thought that. But he had other ideas…ones that didn't include a busy restaurant.

"I figured I'd cook for us. I was going to drive us out to my place, but if you'd rather, we could go to yours. It's closer." And closer was good. Because one afternoon making love to Michelle wasn't nearly enough. "Unless you're afraid to be alone with me."

"Of course not."

He glanced over and she looked truly insulted. "Well, fine. My place or yours? I'll cook."

"Whichever you prefer."

"My place then. I hate to leave Chloe alone all day."

Michelle looked as if she wished he'd said her place, and he didn't blame her. As much as he really did hate leaving Chloe alone, he'd chosen his house because it was his home turf. He hoped that gave him some edge. He needed all the help he could get.

She was quiet the rest of the ride out to his house. And as they went inside and took off their coats and boots, she started toward the kitchen. Rather than following her, he grabbed her hand and gently led her toward the tree. "I made you something. I'll confess, it's sort of a bribe. After you see it, I figure you'll feel you have to ask me to stay for dinner once I help decorate your tree and…well, it will mean I get to spend the day with you both."

"You don't need to bribe me."

"But I wanted to." He reached under the tree and pulled out the small ornament. "Like I told you the other day, my grandfather made an ornament a year for my grandmother. I've kept the tradition, making a new one each year for the tree. I like mixing the new with the old."

Michelle fingered a small birdhouse on Daniel's tree. "I

love that. We never had holiday traditions when I was growing up. I've tried to give some to Brandon."

"Well, we'll make the ornaments a new one for the three of us. So, here's your first one." He handed her the small gift bag.

Michelle opened it up and pulled a small oval Santa's head from it. Daniel had carved and painted it, then added a light stain to give it an antique appearance before he put the sealant on. She studied it. "It's beautiful."

"Did it work?"

"Pardon?"

He wiggled his eyebrows in a particularly wheedling way. "Did I guilt you into inviting me to stay after I help decorate your tree?"

"You look just like Brandon when you do that," she teased. "But yes, after such a lovely gift, I probably have to invite you."

"Ah, there's that enthusiasm again. And speaking of enthusiasm…" He leaned down and kissed her.

She hesitated and pulled back, "Really, Daniel, we…" She let the sentence fade out and kissed him back. Her kiss gave him the answer he was waiting for.

He broke the kiss, laughed as he swept her into his arms, then gave a small grunt. "I always wanted to do it like they do in the movies." He continued grunting and groaning as he carried her to his room.

"I don't think the heroes in the movies make all that noise when they carry the heroine to their room," she assured him.

"That's because they have sound editors who cut that part."

AFTERWARD, wrapped in Daniel's quilt, Michelle snuggled against him. "This is a lovely way to spend a Saturday morning," she told him. "I love being here with you, like this. I know I've been preaching keeping our distance, but—"

He couldn't keep it in any longer. He interrupted her and blurted out what had been on his mind for days, "I love you."

MICHELLE PULLED the quilt tighter and scooted away from him. She was allowing herself to contemplate asking Daniel if they had time to make love again, when he had to ruin it. She didn't know what to say.

After the silence stretched too long, Daniel finally said, "I know you keep saying it's too soon, but I think, if you're honest, you love me, too."

"Samantha said that love doesn't follow a timetable or something like that," Michelle muttered, more to herself than to him. But when she realized she'd said the words out loud, she hastily added, "But even if it doesn't follow a timetable, it's too soon."

"I liked Samantha the moment I met her, and I have to say, she's right. I love you, Michelle. I love everything about you. I love that—"

Before he could list her attributes, she interrupted. "I didn't ask for this. Not for any of this. My life was going along at its own pace. Smooth and serene. Then there you were on my doorstep and nothing's been smooth since."

It was too much. Michelle knew that she didn't handle change well. The last time her life had been this chaotic had been when Tara and Brandon had shown up on her porch. "I want things…"

Michelle didn't finish the sentence. What she'd intended to say was that she wanted things to go back to the way they were, but that wasn't true. She didn't want to go back to a time before Daniel, but she needed things to go slower.

"Maybe you need things shook up."

"Don't you understand—I don't? I like my quiet life. I like the order of it all. And I don't want you to love me." She surprised herself with the last part of her confession. She'd only started to adjust her reality to include Daniel in Brandon's and her life. But love?

It wasn't only the short time they'd known each other. It was the fact that Michelle was pretty sure that loving Daniel would be easy…and maybe that's what scared her most of all.

"Why, Michelle?"

Why? Why did the idea of Daniel loving her scare her more than the idea of him being Brandon's father, or even the idea of sleeping with him? "Everyone I've loved has walked out on me. My boyfriend left when he found out about Brandon. He didn't want to take on the responsibility. And that was fine, but he didn't want me to take it on, either. He wanted us to move to the city and forget about my nephew."

"I'm sorry, Michelle."

"My parents both left me, and Tara. Long before she died, she walked out on me."

"But don't you see, I'm not walking away—I'm walking toward you. You only have to meet me halfway."

Her excuses were lame. Even as she offered the words to Daniel, she knew. "The truth of the matter is, I'm afraid…I don't think I can give you what you want."

"You told me what Brandon said, about how he was what you were meant to do. Do you remember?"

Michelle nodded, the moment one she'd treasure forever.

"Well, maybe I am, too? Maybe I am what you were meant for? Because I'm pretty sure you and Brandon are what I was meant to do."

"Daniel, I don't want to hurt you. I just think we should stop this now while we can. The situation with Brandon and your paternity is tricky enough."

"I'll give you some space so you can—how did you put it?—

adjust your reality. I can't stop loving you because you think it could be inconvenient, but I will back off and give you some breathing room."

"Thanks."

He got out of bed, grabbed his clothes and headed for the other bathroom. "You can have the shower here," he called over his shoulder and he purposely didn't look behind him to see if she was watching his very naked exit.

MICHELLE MADE IT through the weekend, but it was a near thing.

She kept seeing Daniel's very earnest expression as he told her he loved her. She saw it when they picked up Brandon after the tryouts. She saw it as the three of them put up her tree. She saw it as she put the ornament he had made for her onto a branch right at the front.

She even saw it in her dreams. Saw that expression and heard the words again—*I love you.*

By Monday morning she was a wreck. And she couldn't afford to be. There was so much to do for the Christmas Fair. She might have everything in order, but she was exhausted from a weekend of trying not to remember that Daniel McLean had said he loved her.

Samantha burst into the gym, where Michelle was setting up the Chinese auction at the table. "He's not coming."

"Who? Daniel?" Michelle tried to mask her disappointment. She should be relieved. Today was the last day they'd be working on the Christmas Fair. They wouldn't have any reason to be together as much as they'd been the past few weeks. She'd get her breathing room and then some.

"I like that your first concern is Daniel." Samantha sported a very matchmakery smile. "But no, I wasn't talking about Daniel. I was talking about your Santa."

"Mr. Travoetch?"

"Yes." Samantha nodded. "His wife called and he's sick with the flu."

This did not bode well for the day. Michelle's perfect Santa, done in by a bug.

"Now what?" Normally she'd already have formulated a couple alternate plans, but for the life of her, she couldn't manage even one. Dealing with Daniel had turned her mind to mush. She didn't know what to do.

Samantha must have taken pity on her, because she put an arm around her. "You'll just have to find a substitute. There are tons of school dads. One of them should be able to fill in. You go make calls, and I'll keep setting up in here."

Before she left, Samantha asked, "Did you talk to Carly this morning? I called and got her voice mail, so I left a message."

"Me, too," Michelle admitted. "I'm sure she'll call or come over as soon as she's done at the hearing." She was hoping by saying it aloud, she would convince herself as much as Samantha. She felt conflicted, knowing she had to be here but wanting to support Carly.

"Don't worry. Like Carly said, they have a plea agreement all set up. This is strictly a formality." Samantha would have been more convincing if she didn't look so uncertain as she said the words.

"Worrying is what I do best," Michelle admitted. And lately, she'd had far too many choices when it came to topics.

"Me, too. I think it's a mom thing," Samantha admitted.

"Maybe it's an aunt thing, too, because goodness knows, I'm good at it." The image of Brandon getting clobbered by a hockey puck flashed through her mind.

"You're a mom," Samantha said with certainty. "That might not be what Brandon calls you, but you have all the classic signs."

"You can read signs?" Michelle asked.

"Enough to know that not only are you Brandon's mom, you're in love with his possible dad."

There was that word again. Michelle didn't want to talk about love. No, she couldn't. She just wished people would stop pestering her about her supposed love. "I better go make those calls."

She went through the door at the back of the stage, into the hall and practically ran Daniel over. "Oh, you came."

He clutched his heart in mock delight. "Michelle, really, this enthusiasm of yours is becoming embarrassing."

"Sorry, I didn't mean it like that. I'm flustered." Mindful of the potential for kids to overhear, she whispered, "Santa canceled due to the flu. I've got to start making calls and find a replacement."

"Or," he said.

"Or?"

"Or I could do it for you."

She had a hard time picturing Daniel as Santa, but maybe with enough padding, and the beard… "Are you sure?"

He smiled. "Positive. What do you think? Ho, ho, ho."

She didn't have the heart to tell him his Santa chuckle was less than convincing. "I'm sure once we get you in the suit, you'll do fine. Thanks. That's one less thing on my plate."

"Let's go set up and then I'll get changed." He picked up a box that was on the floor.

"What's that?"

He opened the flaps. Inside were dozens of wooden toys. Cars, paddles with balls attached, and some wooden circles intertwined. She picked one up and looked at him.

"A puzzle of sorts. You have to unthread the circles from each other. It's harder than it looks."

She put the puzzle back in the box. "Daniel, these are beautiful, but really, you've already done so much."

"I wanted to, Michelle. And there's so much more I'd like to do."

He gave her a look that told her they were no longer talking about making toys, and she didn't want to have this particular conversation now. "Well, thanks. Now, let's go."

Two hours later, Michelle's volunteers were all there, and the first two classes had come through the Christmas Fair. She moved from table to table, putting out more merchandise for the kindergarten. When she came to the table with Daniel's wooden toys, she brought out a new batch, then glanced in the corner.

Daniel was sitting on the Santa throne, taking child after child on his lap and listening to their Christmas wishes. Connie was manning the camera, snapping Polaroids of each kid, then sending them to the frame station, where Ginny and Diane were helping them frame the pictures in construction paper for their parents.

Julie and Anna were working the beanbag tosses, and there was Dorothy, sitting at the table with the Christmas sucker tree.

Every corner of the room had something of Daniel in it. He'd permeated Erie Elementary as much as he'd taken over so many of her thoughts. She glanced at him again, listening to each child so earnestly. Nodding and giving them his undivided attention.

"Can't take your eyes off him," Samantha said, startling Michelle.

She reached into the box under the table and pulled out a couple more toys, then promptly added them to the rest. "I have to check on everyone and everything."

"Uh-huh." Samantha's tone said what she meant was, *I don't believe you.*

Michelle was about to argue but decided against it, so she changed the topic. "It's been a while. Have you heard from Carly?"

"No. I was hoping you had."

She shook her head. Before she could say anything about how worried she was, Connie was tapping her on the shoulder. "Daniel's taking a break and asked if you would meet him in the coat closet."

"Do we even have a coat closet?" Michelle asked. She'd been involved at the school for four years, and couldn't recall a coat closet anywhere.

"I think he means the locker room." Connie suddenly looked wistful. "But I wish we did have a coat closet. I remember, back in high school, we had one. No lockers then. And there was this redheaded boy—"

Before Connie got lost in the coat closet of her past, Michelle interrupted her and said, "I'd better see what Saint Nick wants."

Michelle walked to the back of the gym and found the locker room door open. She peeked inside and Daniel was there, still dressed as Santa. "Hey, what's up?"

Daniel pointed into the gym. "See that kid?"

Michelle looked at the kindergartners milling about the gift tables. "I see lots of kids."

"The one in the faded shirt." He pointed again.

"Oh, yes. Lincoln White."

"He said he didn't want me—by me I mean Santa—to bring him any toys. He just wants a Christmas tree. His mom said they couldn't have one this year because she lost her job."

"Oh." Michelle hadn't heard that Mindy had lost her job.

"Could you find out where he lives?" Daniel continued. "I mean, not let anyone know why, just get an address?"

She didn't need to ask why. "You're going to get him a tree."

He shrugged, as if it wasn't anything, but it was. It was

something big. And at that moment, Michelle thought maybe her friends weren't as wrong as she thought. Maybe she lo—

"Michelle, hurry," Samantha called. "There's a glue crisis at the craft table."

She wanted to stay. She wanted to tell Daniel about the feelings she was just realizing—no, she'd realized it before, she was just admitting to it now. But she knew she had to go. "Sorry."

"Just don't forget that address."

"No," she promised him wholeheartedly, "I won't forget anything."

She solved the glue crisis and everything seemed to be running smoothly. Everything except Carly. Carly hadn't called her or Samantha.

It was after lunch when she finally arrived. She walked into the gym and Samantha all but pounced on her before Michelle could. "What happened?"

Carly looked exhausted and not nearly as happy as Michelle would have thought. "Carly?"

"There was a bit more to it than we thought," she said slowly, "but it's all fine."

Michelle could see that it was anything but fine. "Carly, we can see it isn't."

"My record will be expunged in a few weeks."

Michelle knew there was more, but it was obvious that Carly didn't want to talk about it. She understood that, so she simply leaned forward and hugged her friend. "Just remember, we're here if you need us."

"I'm fine. Now, where do you want me to work?"

DANIEL WATCHED Michelle with her friends, then went back to his Santa duties.

Playing Santa made the day go fast. The older kids didn't

do any lap-sitting, but when those classes came in, he volunteered at the wrapping station. He had to lose his Santa gloves, but otherwise he was successful.

When the last class had cleared out, all the mothers swarmed the gym, clearing the tables. They had some of the seventh- and eighth-grade boys carry the tables and chairs back to storage.

"Hey, Dan," Brandon said. "Are you going to be here when I get out of school?"

He hadn't talked to Michelle, but nodded. "I should be."

Brandon grinned. "Great. See you in forty-six minutes."

"That's very specific," Daniel teased.

"Hey, I'm Aunt Shell's nephew…and as soon as that bell rings, I'm on Christmas break, so yeah, I'm specific." He took off down the hall.

"What was that all about?" Michelle asked.

He turned, and it took all he had not to sweep her into his arms, right here in front of her friends. "He asked if I'd wait till he got out, and I said I would if it was okay with you."

"When I say yes it's going to be because I have an ulterior motive."

"Oh?" He liked the sound of that.

"I got that address, but I also know the ages of all the kids in the family. I thought we could run to the store and do a bit of Christmas shopping for them, then buy the tree and drop it all off…from Santa, of course."

"I know you don't want to hear it, but I really love you, Michelle. There are so many reasons, but that suggestion pretty much sums them all up." And because he needed to touch her, or burst, he leaned down and planted a very chaste kiss on her cheek. "You've got a date."

Chapter Twelve

At eight o'clock that evening, the three of them ran into Daniel's house with the pizza box.

"I can't remember when I've had so much fun," Michelle said. They'd shopped at Kmart and had all the gifts wrapped at a Toys for Tots wrapping station at the front of the store. There was a tree lot in the store's parking lot, and they bought the biggest blue spruce they could find.

Quietly, under cover of the early winter darkness, they'd brought bag after bag of presents as well as the tree onto the Whites' porch, then Daniel, still dressed as Santa, rang the doorbell, while Michelle and Brandon watched from inside his truck. "You can never tell," she'd warned him.

He'd promised not to. She watched him now, laughing with Daniel as he shoved half a piece of pizza into his mouth. Knowing that Brandon was a soft touch, Chloe was at his feet hoping for a treat.

And Daniel…

Pretty much everything in her life seemed to have an *and Daniel* to it. Not only had he invaded the Christmas Fair, but he'd sort of crept into her entire life. She waited for the familiar sense of fear that always accompanied the thought, but instead, there was something else there. Something warm and sweet.

Something like…love.

As Daniel and Brandon laughed and joked, she knew that this was what she'd always wanted, even when she hadn't known it was what she'd always wanted. She wanted more nights like this.

A lifetime of nights like this.

"Hey, Dan, did you check your mail?" Brandon asked.

All three of them froze. "No, it's the first day that wasn't the first thing I did."

He got up and walked to the front door and, within moments, was back, an envelope in his hand. "It's here." His voice sounded strangely flat.

Michelle felt as if all the oxygen had been sucked out of the room. Once he opened that envelope everything could change.

"Do it, Dan," Brandon said. "Come on."

RATHER THAN TEARING it open, Daniel sat back down at the table. Michelle looked pale, and he understood. "Before we open it, I want to say something."

His hand shook as he set the envelope in front of him and put his folded hands on top of it. He knew these were the most important words he'd ever say. "Listen, whatever is on that piece of paper doesn't matter because I know now what I'm meant to do. Bran, your mom taught me to follow my dreams. And for a while, that dream was the work I do now. And though I still love what I do, I've discovered that it really wasn't my biggest dream. Remember when you told your aunt you were what she was meant to do? Well, you and your aunt are what I'm supposed to do. Being with the two of you means more to me than any job, any project. I want to be your father no matter what this paper says."

"And Aunt Shell?" Brandon asked.

Daniel's gaze caught Michelle's and held it as he said, very clearly, "I want to be her husband." Before she could protest, or even speak, he hurriedly continued. "I know it takes you a while to process things, Michelle. And while I'm willing to wait until you figure out that we are meant to be together, you should know that what I'm planning to do is marry you. Because that's what I was meant to do. The three of us were meant to be a family."

Brandon's grin was the broadest Daniel had ever seen. "It's a once-upon, Aunt Shell."

"A what?" Daniel asked.

Finally, she found her voice. "When Bran first came to live with me, we read together every night. I started with a book of fairy tales I'd loved as a kid. They all started with *once upon a time*—"

"And ended with a *happily ever after,*" Brandon supplied.

"Ever since, when something good happens, we've referred to it as a once-upon."

"Not just really good," Brandon corrected. "Something even better than good. Like if I make the hockey team, that'll be a once-upon. And when you tell Daniel yes, Aunt Shell, that'll be the best once-upon ever." He looked a bit chagrined. "I know, it sounds kind of babyish, but it's one of those things me and Aunt Shell do together. We don't tell anyone."

It was a warning to Daniel that he wasn't supposed to be spreading Brandon's lapse around, but it was also a gift. They'd included him in a private family tradition. "I swear, I'll never tell. Thanks for letting me in on it."

"I knew you wouldn't." In Brandon's voice was a wealth of trust. "And I want us to get a once-upon. That's what Mrs. Williams and Principal Remington got."

"We'll just have to wait for your aunt Shell to make up her mind," Daniel told him. "We're going to have to be patient because it takes her a while—"

"To figure stuff out," Brandon finished.

"Pardon me, boys," Michelle said loudly. "I'm sitting right here."

"Yeah," Brandon said as if she hadn't spoken. "She'll need time to think it through. To make a list. Collect her data. Analyze it. You might have to wait a long, long time, Dan."

"Right here," Michelle said again.

They still ignored her. "I'm willing to wait, Bran," Daniel assured him. "Your aunt's worth it. Us being a family is worth it."

"I don't know why I'm bothering to even talk," Michelle grumbled. "I mean, here I was, about to throw caution, lists and analysis to the wind and say, Yes, Daniel, I'll marry you—"

She didn't get any further than that. Daniel pulled her to her feet, lifted her into his arms and swung her around.

This woman. How could he not have known that his life was missing this woman? "Say it again."

"No lists—" she started.

He interrupted. "No, the other part."

"Yes, I'll marry you. Samantha was right. Love doesn't have a timetable."

Brandon was there, hugging both of them. "This is the best Christmas ever."

"A once-upon Christmas if ever there was," Daniel agreed. "This calls for a celebration."

"The lights are up on Perry Square," Michelle said.

Daniel knew the downtown two-block park well. Each year they decorated the whole thing and the surrounding businesses for the holidays. Multicolored lights. Tons of decorations. And Christmas carols. If anywhere in Erie said Christmas, Perry

Square did. "We could probably stop at Monarch's and get some hot chocolate," he added.

"Double whip cream?" Brandon asked.

"Tonight deserves more than double whip cream. It's triple, at least," Michelle assured him.

"Can Chloe come, too?" Brandon asked.

MICHELLE LOOKED at Daniel. She knew she should be nervous, that her answer meant a huge permanent change, but all she could feel was an overpowering sense of love. A sense that he was right…this was what she was meant to do. Loving Brandon, loving Daniel.

Chloe barked at the sound of her name.

Even loving Chloe. They were a family.

"Sure, she can come," Daniel said. "It's a celebration and she's part of the family."

Michelle squeezed Daniel. Her fiancé.

The word felt strange but right.

She glanced back at the table; the envelope with the test result still sat there unopened.

Michelle didn't mention it. They'd open it later. After all, DNA didn't matter in this case. Brandon had found his father, and she'd found her very own once-upon.

Once upon a Christmas.

Epilogue

Friday, the day after Christmas, Michelle walked into Colao's restaurant, balancing three boxes. Samantha and Carly were both there already in a booth. They'd agreed their Christmas meeting should be all fun, no business. And her announcements were definitely going to be fun.

"Merry Christmas," she cried. She couldn't get over the bubbly excitement that had sat below the surface since Monday. "I have some news. So much news for a mere couple days."

She set the boxes down, pulled off her gloves and extended her left hand, wiggling her fingers in case they missed it.

"Oh, my—" Samantha didn't get any further. She stood and swept Michelle into a huge hug. Michelle hugged her back wholeheartedly. Then she turned to Carly, who grinned. "I told you so."

The waitress walked by. "Hi. Can I get you something to drink?" she asked Michelle.

Carly didn't wait for an answer. "Champagne, please. We're celebrating our friend's Christmas engagement."

"Congratulations," the waitress said, and hurried off.

Michelle slid into the booth. "There's more."

"More than you're engaged?"

"The test result came." She launched into the story, of the

envelope arriving, Daniel's proposal and promise to wait and her own unwillingness to do so. Ending with the hot chocolate and Perry Square. "We didn't open the envelope until we got back."

"And?" Carly asked.

"Daniel is Brandon's father. It sort of seemed anticlimactic, if you know what I mean. After all, we knew that Daniel was Brandon's father, no matter what the test showed."

"Oh, I think I'm going to cry." And with that, Samantha reached for the napkin and started dabbing her eyes.

And that's when Michelle caught the flash. "Oh, Samantha?"

Samantha looked down, then up at Michelle and Carly. "Us, too."

"Jeez, this is turning into a freakin' wedding show," Carly mock-groused as the waitress returned with champagne and glasses. "When dinner's over, bring the check to me, since it appears we're celebrating not just one, but two Christmas engagements."

"And will you be back to celebrate a third?" the waitress teased as she poured the champagne.

"The day I come in and tell you I'm engaged is the day you'll know hell has officially frozen over."

Michelle laughed. "Carly, if you'd asked me a month ago I'd have told you it was never going to happen to me, yet here I am, head over heels."

"And me. If you'd asked me at the start of the school year, I'd have told you I planned to avoid men like the plague. And yet…" Samantha grinned and wiggled her finger at Carly. "Maybe it's the committee. Two of our social activities done, and two of us engaged. And, Carly, I hate to point out, you have the most romantic event of them all."

Carly drained her glass and set it down with a thud, then poured another. "Let me repeat, when hell freezes over."

Michelle raised her glass in a Christmas toast. "To happily ever afters for all of us."

Samantha clinked her glass to Michelle's and Carly followed suit.

"I can drink to that," Carly cheered. "Because I am totally and completely happy in my singleness."

"So, tell us about your hearing," Samantha said. "We've blathered on about happily ever afters and engagements long enough."

"Yes, I'm sorry. You didn't say much at the Christmas Fair. It wasn't so bad?" asked Michelle.

"Well, the hearing didn't go quite the way we thought it would, you see…"

* * * * *

*Find out what happened at Carly's hearing
in ONCE UPON A VALENTINE'S.
Available in February 2009
from Harlequin American Romance.*

Silhouette Desire kicks off 2009 with
MAN OF THE MONTH,
*a yearlong program featuring
incredible heroes by stellar authors.*

When navy SEAL Hunter Cabot returns home for some
much-needed R & R, he discovers he's a married man.
There's just one problem: he's never met his "bride."

*Enjoy this sneak peek at Maureen Child's
AN OFFICER AND A MILLIONAIRE.
Available January 2009 from Silhouette Desire.*

One

Hunter Cabot, Navy SEAL, had a healing bullet wound in his side, thirty days' leave and, apparently, a wife he'd never met.

On the drive into his hometown of Springville, California, he stopped for gas at Charlie Evans's service station. That's where the trouble started.

"Hunter! Man, it's good to see you! Margie didn't tell us you were coming home."

"Margie?" Hunter leaned back against the front fender of his black pickup truck and winced as his side gave a small twinge of pain. Silently then, he watched as the man he'd known since high school filled his tank.

Charlie grinned, shook his head and pumped gas. "Guess your wife was lookin' for a little 'alone' time with you, huh?"

"My—" Hunter couldn't even say the word. *Wife?* He didn't have a wife. "Look, Charlie..."

"Don't blame her, of course," his friend said with a wink as he finished up and put the gas cap back on. "You being gone all the time with the SEALs must be hard on the ol' love life."

He'd never had any complaints, Hunter thought, frowning at the man still talking a mile a minute. "What're you—"

"Bet Margie's anxious to see you. She told us all about that R and R trip you two took to Bali." Charlie's dark brown eyebrows lifted and wiggled.

"Charlie..."

"Hey, it's okay, you don't have to say a thing, man."

What the hell could he say? Hunter shook his head, paid for his gas and as he left, told himself Charlie was just losing it. Maybe the guy had been smelling gas fumes too long.

But as it turned out, it wasn't just Charlie. Stopped at a red light on Main Street, Hunter glanced out his window to smile at Mrs. Harker, his second-grade teacher who was now at least a hundred years old. In the middle of the crosswalk, the old lady stopped and shouted, "Hunter Cabot, you've got yourself a wonderful wife. I hope you appreciate her."

Scowling now, he only nodded at the old woman—the only teacher who'd ever scared the crap out of him. What the hell was going on here? Was everyone but him nuts?

His temper beginning to boil, he put up with a few more comments about his "wife" on the drive through town before finally pulling into the wide, circular drive leading to the Cabot mansion. Hunter didn't have a clue what was going on, but he planned to get to the bottom of it. Fast.

He grabbed his duffel bag, stalked into the house and paid no attention to the housekeeper, who ran at him, fluttering both hands. "Mr. Hunter!"

"Sorry, Sophie," he called out over his shoulder as he took the stairs two at a time. "Need a shower, then we'll talk."

He marched down the long, carpeted hallway to the rooms

that were always kept ready for him. In his suite, Hunter tossed the duffel down and stopped dead. The shower in his bathroom was running. His *wife?*

Anger and curiosity boiled in his gut, creating a churning mass that had him moving forward without even thinking about it. He opened the bathroom door to a wall of steam and the sound of a woman singing—off-key. Margie, no doubt.

Well, if she was his wife...Hunter walked across the room, yanked the shower door open and stared in at a curvy, naked, temptingly wet woman.

She whirled to face him, slapping her arms across her naked body while she gave a short, terrified scream.

Hunter smiled. "Hi, honey. I'm home."

* * * * *

Be sure to look for
AN OFFICER AND A MILLIONAIRE
by USA TODAY *bestselling author Maureen Child.*
Available January 2009 from Silhouette Desire.

CELEBRATE
60 YEARS
OF PURE READING PLEASURE
WITH **HARLEQUIN**®!

We'll be spotlighting a different series
every month throughout 2009
to celebrate our 60th anniversary.
Look for Silhouette Desire® in January!

Collect all 12 books in the Silhouette Desire®
Man of the Month continuity, starting in
January 2009 with *An Officer and a Millionaire*
by *USA TODAY* bestselling author
Maureen Child.

*Look for one new Man of the Month title
every month in 2009!*

SILHOUETTE

SPECIAL EDITION™

The Bravos meet the Jones Gang
as two of Christine Rimmer's famous
Special Edition families come together
in one very special book.

THE STRANGER
AND TESSA JONES

by

CHRISTINE RIMMER

Snowed in with an amnesiac stranger during a
freak blizzard, Tessa Jones soon finds out her
guest is none other than heartbreaker Ash Bravo.
And that's when things really heat up....

*Available January 2009
wherever you buy books.*

REQUEST YOUR FREE BOOKS!

2 FREE NOVELS PLUS 2
FREE GIFTS!

Love, Home & Happiness!

YES! Please send me 2 FREE Harlequin® American Romance® novels and my 2 FREE gifts (gifts are worth about $10). After receiving them, if I don't wish to receive any more books, I can return the shipping statement marked "cancel." If I don't cancel, I will receive 4 brand-new novels every month and be billed just $4.24 per book in the U.S. or $4.99 per book in Canada. That's a savings of close to 15% off the cover price! It's quite a bargain! Shipping and handling is just 25¢ per book, along with any applicable taxes.* I understand that accepting the 2 free books and gifts places me under no obligation to buy anything. I can always return a shipment and cancel at any time. Even if I never buy another book from Harlequin, the two free books and gifts are mine to keep forever.

154 HDN EEZK   354 HDN EEZV

Name	(PLEASE PRINT)	
Address		Apt. #
City	State/Prov.	Zip/Postal Code

Signature (if under 18, a parent or guardian must sign)

Mail to the **Harlequin Reader Service:**
IN U.S.A.: P.O. Box 1867, Buffalo, NY 14240-1867
IN CANADA: P.O. Box 609, Fort Erie, Ontario L2A 5X3

Not valid to current subscribers of Harlequin® American Romance® books.

Want to try two free books from another line?
Call 1-800-873-8635 or visit www.morefreebooks.com.

* Terms and prices subject to change without notice. N.Y. residents add applicable sales tax. Canadian residents will be charged applicable provincial taxes and GST. Offer not valid in Quebec. This offer is limited to one order per household. All orders subject to approval. Credit or debit balances in a customer's account(s) may be offset by any other outstanding balance owed by or to the customer. Please allow 4 to 6 weeks for delivery. Offer available while quantities last.

Your Privacy: Harlequin is committed to protecting your privacy. Our Privacy Policy is available online at www.eHarlequin.com or upon request from the Reader Service. From time to time we make our lists of customers available to reputable third parties who may have a product or service of interest to you. If you would prefer we not share your name and address, please check here. ☐

HAR08R2

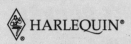

HARLEQUIN®

American ★ Romance®

TINA LEONARD
The Texas
Ranger's Twins

Men Made in America

The promise of a million dollars has lured
Texas Ranger Dane Morgan back to his family
ranch. But he can't be forced into marriage to
single mother of twin girls, Suzy Wintertone,
who is tempting as she is sweet—can he?

Available January 2009
wherever books are sold.

LOVE, HOME & HAPPINESS

www.eHarlequin.com   HAR75245

Silhouette®

SPECIAL EDITION™

USA TODAY bestselling author
MARIE FERRARELLA

FORTUNES OF TEXAS:
RETURN TO RED ROCK

PLAIN JANE AND THE PLAYBOY

To kill time at a New Year's party, playboy Jorge Mendoza shows the host's teenage son how to woo the ladies. The random target of Jorge's charms: wallflower Jane Gilliam. But with one kiss at midnight, introverted Jane turns the tables on this would-be Casanova, as the commitment-phobe falls for her hook, line and sinker!

*Available January 2009
wherever you buy books.*

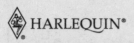

HARLEQUIN®

American ★ Romance®

COMING NEXT MONTH

#1241 THE TEXAS RANGER'S TWINS by Tina Leonard
Men Made in America
Texas Ranger Dane Morgan has been lured home to Union Junction by the prospect of inheriting a million dollars. All he needs to do is live on the Morgan ranch for a year...and marry Suzy Winterstone. While the sassy single mother of toddler twin daughters is as tempting as she is sweet, no Ranger worth his salt can be forced into marriage by a meddling matchmaker! *Can he?*

#1242 MILLION-DOLLAR NANNY by Jacqueline Diamond
Harmony Circle
When her con man ex-fiancé takes off with all her money, Sherry LaSalle finds herself in need of something she's never had before—a job! The socialite may have found her calling, though, as a nanny for Rafe Montoya's adorable twin niece and nephew. The sexy mechanic couldn't be more different than the ex-heiress, but there's something about Sherry that's winning over the kids...and melting Rafe's heart.

#1243 BABY ON BOARD by Lisa Ruff
Baby To Be
Kate Stevens is interviewing daddy candidates. Applicants must be kind, must be stable and must be looking for the same white-picket-fence life Kate has always dreamed of. Unfortunately for her, fun-loving, risk-taking world traveler Patrick Berzani—the baby's biological father—wants to be considered for the position....

#1244 MOMMY IN TRAINING by Shelley Galloway
Motherhood
The arrival of a megastore in Crescent View, Texas, is horrible news for Minnie Clark. Her small boutique is barely making a profit, plus she has the added responsibility of providing for her young niece. So when Minnie discovers that her high-school crush, Matt Madigan, works for the megastore, the new mommy is ready for battle!

www.eHarlequin.com

HARCNMBPA1208